Dangling Gandhi

and

other short stories

Jayanthi Sankar

ZERO DEGREE PUBLISHING

First Edition: September 2019
by ZERO DEGREE PUBLISHING

ISBN: 978-93-88860-03-1

ZDP title no: 22

This is a work of fiction. Names, characters, places and incidents are either the product of author's imagination or are used fictiously, and any resemblance to any actual person, living or dead, events or locales are entirely coincidental.

ZERO DEGREE PUBLISHING
No.55(7), R Block, 6th Avenue,
Anna Nagar,
Chennai - 600 040

Website: www.zerodegreepublishing.com
E Mail id: zerodegreepublishing@gmail.com
Phone : 98400 65000

Writer's Email : jeyanthisankar28@gmail.com/yesjey28@gmail.com

Typeset : Vidhya Velayudham

Cover Art : Chitran Raghunath

Author Photo : Harshita, Singapore

Printed at Repro India, Mumbai

Affectionately, with fond memories
to Ravi-Chitra, Vimal, Vasanth and Priya,...

Contents

Did Churchill Know?

Looking far at the wilds, Jack turned to ask Bala, "Are leeches found here during these months?" when the latter was about to dash up the stairs to go to his house to change.

Tall and slender built Bala halted for a moment, turned around with a broad white smile and said, "No, Sir. Even during the monsoons, we barely get two of them. Leeches are not found within the town," and went in expeditiously.

Standing outside the house near the taxi, Jack looked involuntarily at the nearby bushes. The moist smell of the vegetation around was overpowering. How do leeches in this part of the wilds look and behave, he wondered.

His face had turned a well-ripened tomato red as he enjoyed the warmth of the forenoon. A small patch of loose grey cloud sprinkled a shower - quick and feather-light that stopped even before he could realize it. A couple of friends with their folded up dhoti, deep in discussion, probably berating someone, casually passed by. Their blank straight glances at him didn't last beyond a few seconds.

The room, adjacent to Bala's small humble house, exposing the red-brown bricks, serving more like a kitchen stood without any proper concrete plastering. Behind their home were a few lush banana trees and a large one that looked like a jackfruit tree.

Bala's wife looked out of the window and asked, "*Chaiya edukkatte,*[1] *muthasha*[2]?" The old man, his ebony skin over the stubborn, protruding, old bones, mildly waved his hand and shook his head sideways to say no. She put down his glass and poured tea only into her cup. A thin towel over her tight green blouse, with an ingenuous smile she bent forward to look out of the window.

Bala came hopping back when Jack asked all of a sudden, "I wanted to ask you if you had by any chance come across a group of young Canuck tourists last year? My Annie was with them. I was supposed to join them but couldn't make it because of my mom's surgery."

"Many tourists come every day. So, it's near impossible to remember faces, let alone names," Bala said as he waved to his wife.

"About my age, there were two guys and three girls."

Blinking his eyelids swiftly, with a slight frown, pouting his lips, Bala tried to recollect. "During July, it's normally pouring heavy. Were they into mountaineering by any chance, Sir?"

"They were indeed mountain lovers. Is it true that when leeches bite through our flesh, we don't feel the pain at all?"

"That's precisely why they are all the more dangerous, Sir."

"Yeah! And where are we going this afternoon, Bala? Sorry I digressed abruptly."

1 Chaiya edukkatte – Shall I serve you tea? - In Malayalam
2 muthasha – Grandfather / senior man - In Malayalam

"You could go speed boating. Three days back, you'd said you wanted to experience that landscape once again."

"Okay, I'll think about that. Does your old man always sit in front of the house on the chair like this?" Jack pointed to Bala's grand uncle.

"He waits for any passing jeep to take him to the regional office of *Kannan Devan* Tea. I am not sure if you know, Tata previously owned it. Jeep owners know him well. If there is a vacant seat, they pick him. I do drop him if I happen to go that way. He goes there every day, spends the day there and manages to get a ride back as well."

"Does he have friends there?"

"No, he goes only to reminisce. The first monorail system of India that had served about twenty-two years collapsed in the treacherous floods. The present road just in front of that office is built on the old railway track."

The old man, after a fleeting glance at Jack slowly walked towards the taxi.

Looking into his eyes, Jack greeted him, "Uh what?" in his subtle way.

"*Pathukke*[3]," Bala opened the front door and helped him in.

Hearing his hoarse, phlegmy cough, Jack wondered, "Poor codger must be looking for some residues of his childhood, eh?"

"Something like that, Sir. His father, who worked as a labourer in the tea plantation was washed away in the floods when the rail tracks were completely destroyed. As a four-year-old, he used to wait for his dad daily at the station those days."

"Oh yes! Before I forget, Bala, it's my twenty-fifth birthday on Sunday. We are having a simple party, just the Regency staff and I. Not in

3 *Pathukke* - Slowly/carefully- In Malayalam

such a mood, I tried hard to dissuade them but in the end, agreed. Please do join us," Jack said as he occupied the rear seat. His knees spanned the space between the two front seats.

"*Thonnuththonbathu.*"

"I don't know if I can come, Sir. I need to drive a family from Adimally to the surrounding places," Bala said a little diffidently.

"Come on, just drop by for a while between your busy rides."

"*Thonnuththonbathu.*"

"What's he saying, Bala?"

"Ninety-nine."

"Oh, he understands English! Is he ninety-nine years old?"

"He might look like an irritable boor as he hardly talks to anyone. But having worked under a British tea planter during his younger times, he understands English very well. In another five or six years, he should be turning hundred."

"Then, why does he mutter ninety-nine?"

"1099 as per our Malayalam calendar was the year of the big bad floods. Almost always, he lives in those times."

"An alternate calendar?" Jack asked open-mouthed.

"Yeah, 1099 should be… I think, let me calculate."

"*irubaththulanaalu.*"

"Now it is 1190; then it must be,.."

"English *Kollam irubaththulanaalaanu.*"

"He remembers. The floods were in 1924."

Unbelievingly, Jack looked wide-eyed at the fragile old man's back. The dark grey coat that he wore had many patched up holes that looked as if he was born with it.

"Because of the catastrophic landslide at *Karinthiri,* all the roads were pathetically damaged. About seven years later the present road was built. Worst of all, the church records were damaged beyond recognition. All the present records start only after that. Our ancestors' details are not known. That was one lasting damage caused by the floods."

"So, technically your family tree sprouts from him?" he pointed at the old guy.

"And it ends with him if I can say so because he never got married. He remained a bachelor. His elder sister was my grandma. Both my mother and grandmother were tea plantation workers in those times, and both died of uterus-related issues, common occupational hazard among the women pickers."

Nodding in agreement, Jack looked through the window at the steep valleys and tea estates. The mountains of various sizes touching the horizon intrigued him. The breathtaking views of the wilds and the large, green patches of tea plantations have been haunting him for the past few days even when he slept.

"Grand Uncle is normally very calm. But just a strong passing drizzle could make him coil back into his bed. Once the rains get heavier no one can restrain him. He gets very restless. And like a crazy guy he would start walking in the rain towards the regional office."

"Perhaps, his body has lived and aged over the decades, but his heart perhaps froze in that period, eh?"

How these drivers are impressive in controlling their vehicles on the narrow and steep roads, Jack wondered for the umpteenth time.

"A sure natural skill acquired with long lasting experience, this can be!" he muttered. Bala looked at him in the rear mirror and gave a hesitant, confused smile.

As Bala slid into the town through Munnar-Udumalpet Road, Jack felt yet again the striking contrast between the town and its hilly suburbs. Thanks to tourism, it looked much more contaminated for its size.

When they went past the taxi stand to go beyond, the Catholic Church up the hill with the sculpture of Pope Benedict XVI peered over all the activities of the town, as though monitoring.

The aroma of heated coconut oil crisping raw plantain pervaded the senses. With the roadside hawkers away until evening, the roads suddenly appeared a little broader, he thought.

The loud horns of the autos, buses, and taxis posed a threat to the ears as reckless drivers used the roads both dangerously and chaotically. They seemed to have some method even in the madness. Watching people board government buses to all the four directions Jack was yet again amused to see the locals wearing wooly hats, balaclavas and ear muffs.

Turning to the left, Bala pointed to his right at the cast-iron bridge that extended over the river. He said the old parallel pedestrian Churchill Bridge that stretched parallel to it was built in 1944.

"Did he know?"

"Who?"

"Churchill? That a small bridge here was named after him?"

"I don't know that, Sir. But that's an important historical landmark here in Munnar."

"Okay."

"Churchill was the Premier of the British Empire back then."

"If I may ask, how much have you studied, Bala?

"I passed my BA in history, Sir. But only after three consecutive attempts," he suppressed his laughter.

Looking through the rear view mirror at Jack nodding with an amused broad smile, Bala continued, "That was the most used bridge until a few years ago when people had to wait on both sides to cross as it was too narrow. So, that adjacent metal bridge was installed to ease the human traffic."

"Do you know he hated India and Indians very much?"

"Who?"

"Oh, never mind."

"Aruljyothi bridge across the same river, a little further away, was demolished a few years ago to make way for the upcoming National Highway. Sir, Munnar means three rivers. The town is right at the spot of confluence."

"Bala, are you free tomorrow?"

"I have a ride, but only in the afternoon. Luckily you have come after the rains, Sir. Some mountaineers don't plan properly and choose the rainy seasons. When our folks accompany them as guides, they aren't able to help them much except with the routes and the Mountaineers wouldn't enjoy much as well."

"Climbing in the slippery, rugged terrains could pose a challenge that many love, like my dear Annie used to. She was dauntless."

"It's not just the slippery hills but the leeches that are the worst challenge, Sir."

"I have leech socks with me even if I consider going up the hills. By any chance, did you know the two local guys who went with the group as guides?"

"We can ask around, Sir. It should not be impossible to find out."

"I wanted to walk the roads and paths she had trodden in her last few days. My friends could not help with the names of the guides. Of course, they did give me a group photo with the guides in them. I hope that can help. Is it possible to get any details in the General hospital? I wish to know how painful or peaceful the last hours were for my dear Annie…"

Bala took a look at his face through the mirror.

"Oh, how I miss her!" he muttered to himself.

"I will take you there, Sir."

"After she died, my friends came back, devastated."

"I am sorry to hear that, Sir. Did they take back her body?"

"No, being budget travelers they didn't have the money or the means. They contacted the embassy but for various reasons, though valid ones, even before I could think of flying over to India, the cremation was arranged to take place right here. Having grown up in an orphanage in Toronto, except for me, Annie had no one. I knew her since my high school days and was her steady since then. Even after a year has passed, I am not convinced of this truth, maybe because I didn't get to see her body."

"Sorry, sir..."

"Let's not talk any more of that. It surprises me how even in such mountain ranges devastating floods could have occurred."

"Three weeks of nonstop rains, about 485cm, they say."

"Jesus!"

"Although the accurate guesstimates are unknown, thousands of animals and birds were killed and washed away. Acres of crops and properties were completely destroyed."

“That must have been an unimaginable disaster.”

“What does he do there? I mean at the old station?” Jack pointed to the front left seat.

“Oh, he sits around for some time. Everyone knows him.”

“Poor old fellow!”

“I will drop him there after I drop you at your hotel. He never got to see his father’s body, and he carries the age-old depression and memories. He has never gone beyond these hills, and even today he doesn’t know that open lands exist.”

“How was tea transported during the floods?”

“Not many details are available on the consequences of the halting of tea transport. But those days, tea chests used to be transported through aerial ropeway of about five kilometers from the Top station in Kunadala valley down to Kottagudi.”

“Bottom station.”

“What’s he saying?”

“Kottagudi was called the Bottom station during those times. From there they were transported by carts to Bodinayakkanur, then by trains to various ports to be shipped to England.”

“Bodacious memory he’s got!” Jack muttered before slipping into a silent delving in this own thoughts while looking out at the mystic valleys.

“Sir, excuse me if I sound inquisitive, but, what did she exactly die of, Sir?” Bala asked falteringly.

Jack turned in to look blankly at him for a second. “Oh, Annie died of excessive bleeding caused by a leech bite. One leech had entered her vagina and wriggled right in to rupture the walls of her womb followed by a few internal vital organs before coming out of her abdomen."

"Oh my God! Do you want to go to the Top station?"

"Maybe tomorrow morning, that is if I manage to get up early," laughed Jack as he alighted. The oldster seemed to be staring straight ahead in space, nothing in particular.

Jack bent down to put his hand through the window to touch him and stood agape the moment he saw his shoulders slightly trembling. His cheeks had streaks of freshly glistening wet tracks.

***

Punkah Wallah

Helen checked the large, dark, oblong wooden dining table with a platter of decked toasts, and a half opened a tin of butter from England, hot scrambled eggs, a jug of orange juice, steaming soup noodles, a jug of coffee and a bunch of rightly ripe bananas neatly arranged in the middle.

Winding the thick, strong coir rope around his big toes, Mani got ready to fan the couple while they enjoyed their breakfast. Smelling the aroma, Mani knew he would get to relish his favourite noodles. His taste buds have barely acquiesced to the everyday toasts, even after almost four years.

He would only see Helen's back every day during their meals. Since morning Mani intuitively felt something odd about Mr.Herman. In his pale khaki slacks and full sleeved bright white shirt, he seemed to avoid eye contact with him.

"I am sure Mani can return to Singapore after a couple of months, perhaps with Meena," She told her husband. They always sat facing each other across the width of the table. Mani would never get to lip-read them.

"Just wait, darling, I won't fail you." As he took a bite of his toast he looked up at Mani whose survival with minimum sleep had always remained a wonder for him. With practiced ease Herman, while conversing, making sure his lips were out of Mani's view. He would tilt his head sideways to see Mani's face over Helen's shoulder.

"Come on honey, if we can manage to get electricity sooner, we could get electric ceiling fans installed." She was in her off-white frock with a boat neck and beautiful intricate blue smocking across the chest.

"Trust me, Helen. I shall not forget to think of something."

Giving not just a pleading but also ingratiating expression, Helen widened her honey brown eyes and brows.

About three meter long sheets of about half a meter broad white cloth hung down from the high ceiling, balanced on a set of pulleys fitted on the upper part of it, just above the table in the dining hall. The thick rope that ran down from one end of it was held by Mani's feet. Seated on his wooden bench, he wriggled his toes and feet to stir the dense and humid tropical air. As if ringing a church bell, sometimes, he would choose to pull the end of the rope with his hands gently, but only rarely. The overly ripened bananas, smelling strongly sweet in a bamboo basket on the small table at the corner of the verandah, were attracting swarms of fruit flies. Mani wondered if they were esculent.

"Mani, these bananas, I am sure will help you keep awake. They are for you," Herman had said when he started working for them. Back then, when he was learning to comport himself in the new lands, always hungry, he depended so much on those delicious bananas.

***

It had taken them a month from Negapatnam to reach by steamer. It was a Wednesday. "The city is mourning the death of Queen Victoria," they said. Her Excellency had passed away just the previous day.

"Just twenty-two days into the twentieth century and we hear the first news from back home," said Herman with slight remorse. Unable to decipher the sadness on his face, feeling weak and haggard, Mani walked behind him holding his old and rusty trunk. He had difficulty keeping his attention on Herman's face with various distractions surrounding him. His eyes and mind were overwhelmed by the culture shock of seeing the Chinese and the Malay.

Many rickshaw pullers waited to cater to the strings of alighting passengers. Herman's Gharry, the horse-drawn carriage was waiting for them. Mani boarded with hesitation when Herman tapped him on his shoulder with a smile, saying, "Please get used to the Singapore life." He looked out when Herman pointed to the streets as he talked. Mani read his lips, looked into his eyes and tried to smile as he cringed towards the little window. "You will start liking the city, Mani."

In those initial months, like a fish out of water, he used to feel painfully homesick. Meena used to fill his thoughts mostly. He used to think that he had only one single purpose in life, to make sure his twin sister was well provided.

He had vowed to look after her all her life every time his mother lamented with eyes full of tears, "Who will marry my daughter, so beautiful and clever, yet deaf and dumb?" Chocolate brown skinned Meena with large eyes and long hair looked exotic like the stone sculptures in the Hindu temples.

During his teen years, Mani used to retaliate with welled eyes, his hands flying in all directions and with angry wide-eyed expressions. He used to ask his mother, "Am I not deaf and dumb too?"

Mother would say calmly, "It is not the same for a girl." Only after he left home, he started to understand what she had meant back then slowly.

As the carriage galloped along, Herman showed him around and described to him the fast-growing city. In downtown Raffles Square, most of the roads were red laterite. Raffles place to Collyer quay was the busiest stretch. "Ground floors of the buildings were occupied by stores, and top floor had offices that mostly dealt with imports and some served as godowns." Despite the hot and humid weather, most office goers in the area wore baju tutup.

Several European traders like Behn Meyers & Co, Schmidt & Co, Guthrie & Co were the major ones hoarding on wealth. They needed to sight ships anchoring, and so the companies were mostly along the Quay. Tanjong Pagar wharf was also quite nearby. The local Chinese merchants, born to be traders, mostly were small-scale traders. Some of the locals worked as blue-collar labourers, Herman described to Mani.

Punkahwallahs were employed only by reasonably well off homes and offices. Electricity is a luxury, and most offices had no power or electric fans. Coconut oil lamps were used. Although phones were economic necessities, several offices on the same floor shared a telephone and the telephone number.

Fairly affluent European homes were built, solid rooms with high ceilings surrounded by covered verandahs.

Herman was a hard working storekeeper. He managed a team of assistant storekeepers and coolies. "We import cotton fabric bales." He recollected his formative years when he used to be threatened, "You might have to be sent back to Manchester if you continue to be incompetent."

After a few minutes of complete silence, he would laughingly say, "Eleven years later, now it feels good to look back, but it wasn't any easy those days for me."

Mani observed in the following months that South Indians tended to be either shopkeepers or labourers, notably dockworkers, river boatmen and drivers of the ox carts that were the primary transport for goods to and from the port. North Indians were usually clerks, traders, and merchants. Both groups came to Singapore expecting to return to their homelands and were even more transient than the Chinese. Those who settled longer were in less number. "Nanyang is in constant need of labourers," Herman would say often.

***

Herman came home for lunch as he had not packed with him as he normally would. He ate without talking, just listened to his wife. Showing his back to Mani, he walked around to his wife, bent down to kiss her on her cheek. "Haven't you seen how difficult it was to get a substitute, a temporary one for a couple of weeks when Mani fell ill last year? And it was near impossible to find a deaf person."

"But how long will you keep saying that?"

"We're lucky to have gotten Mani from a decently familiar background to suit our privacy. Do you know how personal matters leak through these fan guys? Mr. Fernandez has told me many stories. His punkah wallah who could hear also understood English. That guy told him everything about his wife who cheated on him."

Wiping his mouth with his napkin, Herman got up from his seat. Herman waved both his hands like the spread wings of a huge bird to attract Mani's attention before making blinking actions with his ten fingers. Mani nodded his head, got up from his seat and bowed slightly.

"So Mr. Fernandez bothers only about the punkah wallah carrying tales?" She followed him as he walked to their bedroom.

"I suppose that mattered to him a lot more," he mumbled.

"Our Mani is not like those idiots. He would never do such things even if he could hear and talk."

"I know that as well, Helen. Let's see how this can be sorted out."

"But the poor guy needs to go to his sister, can't you understand? He loves her like his own life. Tell him about your brother's letter. Let him go now. Call him back later if you wish."

"Let's discuss this during dinner, please."

"As you wish. I heard Fernandez's have electricity now."

"Yes," he answered in a word as he took his hat from the closet.

Hearing the persistent cries of the infant, Helen rushed to the nursery to attend to it.

Just then Mani caught the hand reaching for the bananas. All astir, Meng managed to grab four bananas and burst out laughing and slapped Mani on his back.

Mani turned around and smiled broadly showing his sparking set of white teeth. "*Makaan*[4]?" Meng asked him gesturing with his fingers. Bright-faced Mani shook his head, not yet.

Exactly ten minutes later, Mani was helping Herman carry his office suitcase to the Gharry. It was drizzling slightly. "Mani, please help Helen later. She expects guests in the afternoon." Mani nodded and suddenly remembered that he had to change the fan cloth. He ran a few steps ahead of Herman. "That can wait until tomorrow afternoon. I am sure."

Mani walked towards the house, looking at Meng who hesitantly ambled towards Herman.

When the intransigent Herman looked up, "What brings you here today?" Meng just smiled without a word.

"Who is the other lad?"

"Duan is a *sin kheh*[5]. He needs a job, Sir."

4 Makaan? - Food? (in Malay)

5 Sin Kheh - A hokkian word to address a recent immigrant, who knows nothing about the local rules or Madarin or other languages except his dialect, from China.

"What can he do? And how old is he?"

"He is sixteen, and he can be a coolie."

"He looks hardly eleven! Will he cut off his pigtail? I doubt." Herman pointed at the long thin pigtail running from the nape of his neck to touch his waist. More than half of his shaven front scalp shone in the afternoon sun. His black trousers were unevenly folded to show part of his calf muscles on both the legs. He wore a shirt, without a collar, which had almost lost its original whiteness.

Laughingly Meng looked at his new friend. "I shall tell him to cut it off, Sir."

"Persuade him and do that first. I doubt if he will budge. Meanwhile, I will put in a word to Mr.Chen but let me tell you, and I can't guarantee him a job."

Meng stood there nodding his head.

"Come next Saturday to give me a cut, will you? And don't send your assistant like the other time."

"Certainly Sir," he bowed and left. The boy went after him.

The lad had a scar that looked like a severe cut, on his arm. Mani ran his fingers through the long deep scar below his own right calf muscle. He was yet again reminded of the unforgettable incident in his mid-teens.

***

Mani's father died when he was about fourteen. It was so sudden that it shattered his mother. She had no support whatsoever from her parents' side. Her only brother Murugan, who had sent a sack of rice as a help, lived in a village near Nerur. The neighbours used to sympathize with his mother. "How is she going to survive alone with the twins?" As a widow, she had to stop going out of the house. It was unacceptable for Mani to see her in a white sari - without ornaments or the red vermillion mark on her forehead.

With hair oiled and parted in the middle, rotund Murugan, his uncle, visited them after two months. His mother wondered why he had come but humbly hosted him by cooking the vegetable that she had previously reserved for her children. "Of course, I shall leave only after dinner," he had generously announced.

When Murugan took out a few cheap but new clothes for the two of them, his mother thought her brother was being kind. Meena and Mani were studying for their exams then. They were in the seventh form. But for the mats and a few belongings, the almost empty small room smelt of sesame oil from the mild fumes arising from the little lamp.

"I have meant to ask you about something, but I hesitate," Murugan started.

"*Enna annaa*? Please ask."

"I thought if you can let me adopt your son, I will give this small house to you and your daughter. I will make proper documents. So, you can stop paying me the rent right away. He will be my only son and inherit all that I have including the big house I live in." Married for several years, he had no offsprings.

Mani's mother was shocked at first. Never did she expect him to say such words. She did not answer him. "I am pinning all my hopes on Mani to take care of us."

"I can adopt any other better and younger child, but I thought by doing this I would be helping you, my only sister."

Mani noticed that his mother did not say no. Nor did she agree. She was calmly listening as she cut the vegetable. Trying to lip read, Meena and Mani were watching, looking at each other now and then.

"I will continue to help you both, but only you should never claim your son back."

"Can't I even see my son?" Mother asked chokingly.

"Adoption will have to be done legally."

When his mother did not disapprove of the idea, Mani felt she was getting ready to give him away. Feeling deceived, he thought he would've felt a little comfortable if she had immediately refused Murugan's request.

Unexpectedly, in an impulse, Mani walked out of the house in a flash and absconded for the next few days. No one was able to stop him nor trace him later. His mother cried inconsolably.

On the fourth day, Mani was escorted home by a police constable. "*Dorai ungala naalaikki vara sonnaaruma*," he said to Mother who stood behind the half closed door.

"But why?" mother was terrified to hear.

"Don't worry. English officer is a kind person."

Mani's calf muscle was severely injured. They had nursed it and bandaged the leg. "Don't worry, that will heal soon. Your son was sleeping with this wound in the wild. We rescued him while patrolling. His fever has reduced now."

A week later, the neighbour took Mani along to meet the officer. "He wants to send your son with his brother to Singapore to work as a punkah wallah. I think it is an excellent arrangement as he will earn far better wages. Don't refuse. This boy will have a bright future," he said upon returning.

Mani readily agreed. He didn't mind parting with Meena, but he would not agree to be given away in the name of adoption. Then all arrangements for Mani to leave were made by Herman, who was as kind as his brother. Instantly, Mani liked Herman with the cropped copper coloured hair neatly combed with a left parting.

***

Mani seated himself in the verandah adjacent to the dressing room. The curtains were drawn, leaving a small gap just for the fan rope. He started pulling the fan rhythmically.

Ladies arrived one by one in their respective coaches and cars and gathered in the hall. Mrs.Herman came near Mani and gestured to him to start on the other fan. He nodded, stood up bowed and went near the entrance.

"Can I take that seat, please," Mrs.Chen vied for the single sofa that showed its back to Mani. "Don't worry, he is deaf," Mrs. Nair said.

"I don't want him to read my lips," Mrs.Chen said.

"Mani is a nice boy," Helen gently corrected her. She looked ravishing with light makeup, cherry red lipstick and in her flowing gown matching her hair.

"The town hall looks magnificent after the renovation, doesn't it?"

"It's Victoria memorial hall."

"Oh! I should get used to the new name," they giggled together.

"Cholera break down has claimed 756 lives. The health care system desperately needs a revamp," criticized Mrs.Chen.

"That's a passing cloud. I am more concerned about the Opium inhaling. What a constant cancerous headache it has become!"

"Well, think about it this way. For the little money the Chinese coolies slog for, they need to relax too," Helen said.

"And members of the secret society mint money out of that. They also make good use of their financial crises."

"And who creates the crises or runs the gambling dens?" Mrs. Ali demanded.

"Agreed, it's a vicious circle," Mrs. Nair said drawing a big circle in space.

"What a big threat they are to the straits government!"

"The British government!" Helen corrected with a burst of childish laughter. Her blonde curls bounced as she shook.

"Stand corrected. And I heard the Tongmenghui is founding a branch in Singapore. Collection of donation has begun," said Mrs. Ali, the wife of the public works department employee.

"It's high time Motorcars are commercialized here. Look at Hongkong!" Mrs. Wong changed the topic instantaneously.

"It can solve all the traffic problems of this growing city. Rickshaws are becoming a real menace."

"I differ here. Only public trams and buses can help Singapore."

"I hear it's an offence henceforth to employ a singkeh because the officials have to depend on the owners to explain the rules to them, which seldom happens."

"So many stories on the latest strike, I have been following. Residents in many areas could not get rickshaws. Everyone walked."

On the day of the significant kerfuffle rickshaw strike, the city looked as if plagued. The primary mode of transport within the central and the outskirts came to a standstill.

"This is how Singapore would have been fifty years back, all deserted," people awed. Rickshaw pullers and bullock cart drivers refused to go on the streets. "Imagine having to pay five dollars monthly tax!" the rumour spread all over the island like a forest fire.

Various community heads ordered to stop business on Saturday. Bakers and hawkers shut down shops to avoid further losses.

The Hengwah organised the strike and Hokchia rickshaw owners of Queen Street and Victoria Street to oppose the government's idea of imposing simple road safety rules like: keeping left, not to cut across in front of the horse pulling carriages, not to rush furiously around corners or across roads to pick their prospective passengers, to stop when policeman holds his hand up. Except for a few private rickshaw pullers, all had joined in the strike.

"Evoking the license will affect the owners, not the pullers." Any licensed rickshaw seen functioning were pulled and smashed by Samseng, people said. They stoned the pedestrians, bicycles, and carriages along Tanjong Pagar Road and New Bridge Road.

The strike spread wider by evening, and the police were ordered to carry pistols.

"Empty rickshaws should return to the nearest stand. They can't be crawling about the traffic."

Thousands of rickshaws, day and night, thronged the busy streets and posed a danger. Increasing the monthly tax for rickshaws to three dollars like in Hongkong would undoubtedly work. The officials thought the number of rickshaws should decrease subsequently. The next day the pullers refused to cooperate. It rained heavily. With pistols, Sikhs were stationed at intervals along Orchard road which looked all empty.

"Our Singapore's place has become more important for the British Empire now."

"And it seems after several years, the straits dollar has just started picking up value."

"That's why important public works are expected to begin soon," Mrs. Ali said.

"The city building is speeding up, and it seems Governor Sir John Anderson plans to bring more Tamil convicts from the prisons of Madras province soon to work in the brick kilns, is that true?"

"Authentic news," Mrs. Ali said with conviction.

"If not for the floating population of the cheap Chinese coolies, I can't possibly think of any growth in this city."

"I heard from reliable sources that the Chinese comprise almost half of the island's population."

Oblivious to the ladies' chattering, Mani continued to pull the fan. Mani had on his lap an old newspaper which he tried to read slowly. Thinking of Meena brought tears into his eyes. Mani resigned himself to the cruel fate after her marriage three years back. He'd cried for days after reading the letter that had arrived, and refused to go to India.

"What's the point?" he had asked in reply to Herman's persuasions. He sent his wages home more diligently than before.

***

As usual, as the only fairly well-read person in the small village, Mani's uncle, who was the village head, was given the job of a postmaster. If that post were to be legalized as a branch office, then a proper salary would have to be paid. So it was just an honorary post.

They received not even three or four letters a day. So, only once or twice in a month only would be a few more posts. But the runner would come religiously every day from town as letters had to be dispatched out from the village.

"You are twenty-seven years older than her," Mother had said hesitantly in a low voice. "You are not even my younger brother but elder to me by several years."

"Oh okay, you are free to get a young, handsome groom. I am not stopping you."

"Just because my child is a born,.." mother mumbled with a chock.

"I can get a second wife from the next village. There are a few ready families. Can't you see I am trying to help you by marrying your daughter," he'd said.

"I will think about this."

"If she can bear me a child, I don't mind marrying that deaf and mute girl of yours," Murugan had said pointing to Meena. "Now that I will get a son of my own, ask your son to return home. I shall make him a runner. He will get a regular income."

"If I had a child would I even think of marrying again?"

Mother had no choice but to marry off Meena to him. After two years, Meena also ended up childless.

***

During dinner, after describing her afternoon to her husband, Helen gently twisted her body to take a look at Mani. He looked nothing more than a silhouette.

"I always wonder how Mani thinks. Does he have his language?"

For a second Mani thought they might be discussing him.

"Maybe as images or just abstracts?" Herman said seriously.

"I have wished to ask him sometimes," she said.

Herman laughed loudly. It was not clear if Mani was awake or half asleep. The fan above was moving but slower, cautiously, not to put off the four large candles that illuminated the dining hall. "I shall put away these two chicken drumsticks for Mani. He loves them."

Getting into a serious mood, Herman said, "Thought itself is not a language, and I believe that's the reason language always produces errors in any communication. That's why ancient Greek philosophers always said you must define your terms before engaging in any conversation."

"I hope to understand that better one day. How is Meena?"

"With lack of activity, the post master's health has worsened, and he has been bedridden for weeks. Meena is patiently taking care of him, my brother says."

"All the properties including farmlands bought by Mani's earnings are being taken away by the first wife and her folks. That's my concern right now."

"Please ask your brother to help Meena, Herman."

"I have already told him. But, how much can he do?"

"You need to disclose to Mani about the letter you hid last year. He is not even aware that his mother is no more."

"I don't feel any good about what I've done, but I feared that we might not have Mani at a crucial time when you were about to have our baby during May. And you know well enough how Singapore can get during those months."

"Now his sister is widowed, all alone there. She needs Mani, her only next of kin."

"I agree. I hope electricity reaches our home before Mani prepares to leave us. Shall we window shop for our ceiling fan this weekend?"

"Yes. Make arrangements for Mani's departure with someone genuinely trustable."

"I will do just that for all his service to us for these six years."

"And I hope to have the twins back with us at the earliest. He could even marry and bring along his wife."

"But, do we still need a punkah wallah?"

"Maybe not, but they can help us in other ways. Our household can always do better with two women, and assiduous Mani can be an asset in your office."

"We shall have to think about those things later."

After Helen left, Herman sat alone at the dining table for long, staring straight at Mani first and later slouching to gaze at the candle flame and then for a few minutes eyes closed, holding his head in his hands.

Although Mani at first felt strange seeing him that way, he soon ignored that and relaxed. As he was solemnly pulling the rope, he failed to notice Herman get up from his seat.

Herman stood watching him. A few times Mani's head fell forward, but he continued to pull the rope.

Herman came near him to gently touch his shoulder. "Can I have a word with you, Mani?"

A little puzzled, suddenly aflutter, shrouded by fear Mani got up hurriedly leaving the rope behind and went after him.

Herman took the envelope from the drawer. With a forced but kind smile, "No, fear not. As always, I have no complaints whatsoever against you, Mani," He slowly pronounced every word facing him as he pulled out the letter.

***

Peacock feather fan

When the Deputy Editor called his line, "Could you please come to my cabin for a moment?" Roger left a sentence typing halfway, logged off, threw his hands upwards to stretch his thin and gaunt physique before walking towards her cabin.

He knocked and entered. "Take your seat. The editor had called me to check if the story on the animal lover has shaped. She says it had to be published within the next few days."

"Ya, in fact, I've already started ideating the story. David has taken brilliant shots of Lisa with her pets," Roger said benignly.

With hair that looked interestingly bristly with a recent close crop, she looked younger and more immaculate, in her formal navy blue dress, he thought.

"Since it's our feature, Editor said that we might think of a catchy blurb in the 'Island times' and also to inform Wendy that you will have your first byline in this," the Deputy said looking straight into his eyes.

He controlled his jubilance at that and just smiled as he proceeded to debrief on the assignment.

As an animal lover, Lisa gave her opinion on the missing cats of Khatib. Facing the camera, Lisa had melted, "The animals are not like humans, they can't possibly ask for their rights, you see?" cautiously feigning to touch her mascara laid eyes. She had two cats, a dog and a couple of hamsters. "When I heard about the serial cat killer I cried and cried the whole, you know. I hope the police can find the guy soon. *Can or not?*"

Almost in tears, Lisa said, "It's already a sin you know when people abandon their cats and dogs. I can't imagine someone is killing them one by one. Poor things, I *can not taahan any more lah*[6]. Please do something, Police!" She tried to speak on the positive side when she said, "I like what 'ACRES' is doing, helping in so many different ways to treat and shelter the estranged and confiscated animals of all kinds."

"I have three young children who always love to watch national geographic. But, I leave them in the neighbor's house because I can't watch animals killing each other," she showed her hand towards the living room window. "She was so happy to get featured making it an opportunity to show her gratitude she had made chicken rice for us. And she had originally planned mutton curry and fish ball soup to treat us all, she said."

Wrinkles formed on her forehead as she frowned slightly.

"All the best for your story," the Deputy said indicating that he could leave. "Better not get personally involved with such contacts while on work visits."

He nodded as he exited.

Roger went near Wendy's and smiled, "How is your Sunday feature shaping?"

6 I can not taahan any more lah – I can't take it anymore

"Not bad."

"An old woman called me for the third time in a fortnight to plead 'Can you look for my cat?'"

"Oh dear!"

"The first time when she had called I told her I am just a reporter cum editor, not a policeman. But I was astonished when she told me to buy fish porridge on my way to her house."

"Really? Maybe she has no one to seek help."

"But I wondered since when have our cops become errand boys?"

"But how did she get your number?"

"That puzzles me as well. But I guess this number previously belonged to a police guy because this is not the first time that I was called with an assumption that I'm a cop."

"You could have guided her to call the actual police," she looked deeply into his eyes.

"She didn't let me talk at all, you know. She went on saying she lived in Yishun and that her name is Aziza, and that she is eighty-three years old but would keep repeating in between - please look for my cat."

Wendy's line rang. Picking the call, she gestured towards the Deputy's cabin. "Catch up later," waved and glided off.

The Deputy looked at Wendy as if she was seeing her for the first time. She moved an A3 print out of the page in progress towards Wendy. "It's like a slap on my face!"

Bewildered and confounded, Wendy stood open-mouthed for a second before saying, "I don't understand what you mean."

"When I am here, telling you to use the text I had sent you, you are supposed to use only that. Why did you do your own editing?"

"Sorry, I still don't understand."

"I spent time editing that advertorial, you know."

"Oh, okay. But I was not aware of that."

"But you seem to have used the original text to edit yourself."

"I received two internally forwarded emails. I still don't understand how this happened. Let me think."

Suddenly, Wendy realised that the Deputy was looking not at her but at her sandstone necklace.

"I don't want to hear any of your stories."

"But you will slap me with your words?" she muttered to herself.

"Beg your pardon?" the Deputy looked at her with a glare.

"I said I deserve an opportunity to explain, at the least."

"But I have a lot to finish," she spread her palm and showed her files on the table before placing her elbows with a deliberate gait. She folded her hands leaning on the table.

"I just remember now, and I received a forwarded attachment of the same from Mr.Tan the same day."

"But why take from that attachment when I have sent you mine?"

"Well, I thought since they are the same,..." Wendy tried to explain.

"No, they were, don't assume. My point is that I spent time editing and it defeats the purpose."

"Precisely, in fact, I would have preferred to use the text you edited to save my time and efforts."

"Then why didn't you?"

Feeling implacable, Wendy zipped her mouth.

"And why didn't you edit the other text on the community event?"

"I thought you had vetted Mr.Tan's edits."

"You must edit where ever necessary."

"Ok," she said almost inaudibly, "And perhaps get 'kicked' by him for a change, instead of getting slapped."

"What did you say?"

"Nothing," she foozled.

"You said something."

"Well, I said, from now I shall clarify with you daily as to which ones I should be editing and which ones I should not be editing."

"But you are the editor of the page, aren't you?"

"I think so. Or am I?"

"When I send, use them as they are. Any other texts you receive, please edit suitably."

Wendy came out fuming. They just exchanged eye contact, and Roger knew from her flushed face not to ask her anything for some time.

Roger watched her hurriedly checking her mobile. He waited for her to finish the serious conversation that lasted for a few minutes. Then he went near to ask, "Anything wrong, Wendy?"

"Nothing wrong. It's just that my younger doll had a fever this morning. But she is fine now and playing, and it seems, I just checked with my domestic help."

"Aziza had called again," he said thinking that she looked more tired than usual.

"Roger, why don't you take it as a mission to look for her cat? Poor Aziza," she laughed mildly.

"Come on, am I Murakami's Nakata?"

"How is your grandma's roaches problem now?"

"Oh, she said cockroaches anyway return after some time. That's the price we pay for the low-level flats, priced lower. It seems there is less number of cockroaches recently. She is allergic to sprays, and so we had to shift her to our house before spraying her whole house a few months back. And she has recently spotted a few lizards, and she is terrified of them now."

"They must have been feasting on the roaches," Wendy beamed broadly.

The Deputy peeped out of her cabin to call Roger. Not expecting to be called again, he hurried to her cabin. He noticed that Mr.Tan, in his beige polo and brown denim pants, was already seated there. With an awkward care avoiding glancing at him, he sat looking at the Deputy. He felt the air heavy. They seemed to have had a long argument or some serious issue.

"HDB is investing 45 dollars in its new project," lampooned the Deputy throwing on the table before him the page folded to show the two-column news. Nonplussed, he kept quiet.

"The very first sentence has the 'million' missing." Roger was shell-shocked. His brain seemed to have stopped functioning.

"Why don't you say something?" her propensity, as usual, had put him into silence.

"Sorry," he tried to mumble with despair in his eyes and voice.

"It's almost a year since you joined, I think."

"I complete one year next month," he said feebly.

Deputy's smile looked hideous to him when she said, "And you could make such a factual error. I need to talk to your mentor, Wendy, on your nescience."

"Mr.Tan was on duty that day. Not just that, he was the final proofreader of the page as well," in remorse he searched for the best suitable words but almost failed.

"Stop pointing fingers at others. Be happy that you are not thrown out immediately as we normally do for such blunders. Carelessness as yours can be perilous. Do you know what it can be to answer the respective officials?" she asked with a controlled but ferocious hiss.

"I was doing my page with a severe migraine that day. I desperately needed help, and I got none. Mr.Tan stopped helping me totally except searching for an image or two. Subsequently, everyone started to follow him. And that left me with no help."

Both looked aghast.

A warning letter was issued. With a pale face, Roger walked out of the room languidly.

Roger went straight to Wendy and showed. With repugnance, he lamented, "They had typed, signed and kept it ready. Isn't this verdict without investigation?"

"Hush, and easy."

"I thought Mr.Tan was a Senior Sub Editor. Since when has he become the Accuracy Editor? Did we ever before have such a post in our office?"

"But we have it now, don't we? A new incarnation. Someone has to become the scapegoat. And who will that be? Most junior in the team, or contract staff," she smiled broadly, but he didn't.

"But,..."

"Come on, Roger baby."

"Will this affect my annual appraisal? Having worked here for more than ten years, you should know well."

"Why worry about that now?"

"But all the blame is thrown on my shoulders," he sulked.

"That's how it is mostly. It's teamwork just in name. As soon as an issue arises, each will put self before others. That's the basic rule everyone follows."

"He interacts so warmly, and I have felt him treat me like his own son. And to think he didn't even utter a single word to her."

"I know how you feel. Don't fall for the urbane manners. Everyone learns from the past and applies his experiences the same way when they get their opportunity."

"It's not as if I have never seen people in my life. I am not from an alien planet. But these open, intricate, direct, indirect shades of politics overwhelm me. If it is a mistake committed or carelessness then shouldn't the magnitude remain the same irrespective of whose it is?"

"Been there and seen a lot of that."

"But,.."

"In the power race, the fittest survive. The upper hands would do anything to save their asses. Creating a completely new abstract position is absolutely nothing, though this is entirely new to me as well. Face the fact, but cheer up. Don't be such a milquetoast," she said.

"Today, I voiced my stand, Wendy."

"Oh good, I think you will be fine after you sleep it off tonight," she said patting hard on his shoulder. "Time for our meeting," they scurried along with the others.

During the Editorial, Roger was not his usual self. Ahmed bent down to ask in his ears, "Are you unwell?" He just shook his head to say no.

In the local section, the serial cat killer getting 18 months supervision took center stage discussion. "It seems that guy was mentally ill. The noisy cat had made that 41 year old get furious, they say. He came out of his house, lifted the cat that was trying to go up the stairs to the second level. Holding the cat, calmly he went up the elevator to the thirteenth floor and threw it on the ground from there," Ahmed elaborated.

Mr. Tan tried to contribute, "There has been a string of feline deaths. Since October, seven cats were dead in twelve days."

"Check if the images are embargo and remember to add the byline. I think the image credit goes to the police. You may show me a print out at the earliest for me to have a look at the layout," the Deputy said.

"If there is any breaking news this will go in. We will decide that later. As of now, this is the first page lead of the section. And it goes into the top attraction of tomorrow's issue, don't forget."

When Mr. Tan said to Roger, "I don't have an assignment today, please help him with the story," he simply nodded in affirmation. He didn't look at him more than a second.

"Wendy, please spare me a few minutes after the meeting," Mr. Tan said as he got up to exit. Once the 'local section' team along with the reporters came out, the 'Asia section' team filled the room.

When Samy started raking, "PTI says a tigress was killed in the Soopkhar range of the famous Kanha Tiger Reserve in a suspected territorial fight with another feline, a forest official said today," everyone's attention focused on him.

"Was it a man-eater?"

"I don't think so. Earlier on, in South India, a tiger was shot for having killed three women over two weeks," Samy added. Looking deeply into his face the Deputy gave a hostile nod without the slightest croak.

"And last week, Menaka Gandhi criticized the minister for the 'go ahead' to shoot the nilgais. As per India's Wildlife protection act 1972, she argues that vermin like rats, crows and termites can be exterminated but not the endangered species."

"Samy, could you stick to the current story? Why connect all that comes to your mind and slant the story?"

Unyielding as always he said, "We could add some background. And I thought this story could develop further and there could be some possible follow-ups this week."

Her frown said she didn't like his idea. "Remember to check with other sources as well."

"Shall we have an exclusive page for cats?" Suddenly, Samy tried to ease the atmosphere. "Cat page!" Laughter filled the room. "Enough of the rhetoric," Deputy barged in to stop the amusement. The hubbub subsided instantaneously.

The Asia team spilled out with all the hustle and bustle.

Wendy went to Mr. Tan's desk. He was sulking to someone over the phone, "Oh she holds a post so decorative that even the weekly editorials are to be always written only by me. I think it could help to have a framed photo of hers on the wall here as we almost forget her face these days," The moment he spotted Wendy he wrapped up the conversation abruptly saying he would be busy the whole afternoon.

"I just wanted to tell you please don't edit the community event text I attached to you because they want an extensive coverage. The organisers had called me in the morning."

"Did you discuss it with her?" she showed the Deputy Editor's cabin.

"No, I haven't, and I don't intend to."

"Then I will go with a printout and check with her first," Wendy said smilingly trying to sound normal as she left.

He just gave her a villainous look behind her back.

Around five when Wendy came to his desk and said, "Shall we go for a coffee?" Roger was checking his emails.

"Aziza's is one of the few dozen cats missing, and I don't know how to explain it to her?" Roger said. Wendy didn't respond but gave a 'poor thing' expression.

Roger kvelled within himself when she said, "Your layout stood out, I'd say. I will read through soon," and wished that at least this time his story doesn't get killed with some inevitable coverage of some breaking local news.

"I left my mobile charger at Lisa's house. I had been there yesterday. She was away to the vet with her pets, but she had left my charger with her neighbour. Lisa's children, all below seven, were there."

Wendy listened with occasional nods.

"Leaving the children to play on the floor in the common corridor in the afternoons, Lisa stays inside the house with her pets. The father who works in Batam comes once in a fortnight. Seeing the children having ant bites all over their bodies, he would reprimand her, and they both end up fighting. She would scream at the top of her voice and wouldn't let him touch her pets. The irony is we are going to feature her as an animal lover."

"We are not here to change the society — media matters, but always remember we can only report. Be happy that you have another contrast angle to cover when the appropriate time comes."

"But I don't wish to. I wouldn't be allowed to anyway."

Both of them turned to look when Samy joining a group announced happily with boisterous laughter, “And now all the cow, goat, chick eaters head fast towards the canteen.”

Walking behind them, Wendy turned with a smile, “My cousin says that you can ward off lizards using peacock feathers. You can buy a fan from one of the shops in Little India. It would be a good wall ornamental item for your granny’s living room. No harm in trying.”

“But then, will the roaches return?”

She halted to look blankly at the floor for a few seconds and wide-eyed she shrugged her shoulders as she continued to walk with an easy smile at him.

***

Mobile dictionary

I

David was seated on a chair in the small study adjacent to the pyol of the red-tile-roofed ancestral house. Ramasamy opened the window. The morning rays of the sun unfolded the interior. Pigtail bundled into an elongated bun tugged away into his white turban, with his *Panjagacham*[7], and faded black coat over his dull white shirt, three lines of holy ash smeared across the forehead with a vermillion dot in the middle he was ready to leave for school, the only high school in Periyakulam.

The wooden bookshelf mounted on the wall contained some classics and several versions of the English dictionary. "Why do you care so much for this when you have them all up there?" David showed the dictionaries first and then his temple with his index finger.

"My descendants might appreciate the edition. Or so I hope. Thank you for the treasure. I'm honoured." Mr.Ramasamy carefully put away the dictionary in its clear pouch before placing it on the shelf.

7 *Panjagacham*- longer white dhoti wrapped in a special way with five insertions.

"My cousin, waiting to be posted, arrived last week from Birmingham. He had a copy that he was willing to part with. By the by, could you please,..?"

"The meaning or the spelling?" Ramasamy laughed boyishly.

Joining in the laughter, David piqued, "Tell me the meaning of the word 'epeolatry' please." He was combing his dark brown waves of hair with his long slender fingers.

Ramasamy closed his eyes jauntily for a couple of seconds. "Worship of words."

Eyes full of admiration David asked, "Fen?"

"Swamp," came the immediate reply.

"Thank you Mr.Dictionary," David said admiringly widening his blue-grey eyes. "At last after eleven days of hunger strike, Bose has been released and put under house arrest, I hear," he switched to politics.

"Yes, I heard it on the radio," Ramasamy said.

"I think the hero deserved at least that much of dignity."

"Indeed, but I can't comment more on that," he laughed.

"Why?" David teased as he admired yet again his childlike laughter.

"As you know well enough, I am a government employee."

"For aught I know, I'm one too."

"Evidently," he laughed again. "But are we the same?"

"Do you know something? One of my colleagues asked if you were my mentor, and I spontaneously said yes." Ramasamy smiled at the puerile statement as he went in to give the coffee cups, "Neela, please wash this china and keep them away safely on the rack," he said. His sister appeared seraphic, draped in an off white sari walked towards him.

In the darkness, with black curls on the sides of her forehead, her sharp-nosed, large-eyed face glowed like a gentle flame of an oil lamp.

David inserted a cigarette size rolled paper rolled to fit in between the gap in the window pane as he said aloud, “I take leave Mr. Ramasamy. Many thanks for the coffee.”

***

Ramasamy was inclined to make more money to provide better for the family. He was now barely making ends meet with his monthly salary. Lakshmi, their cow, always better fed at home, received the lion’s share in the monthly budget and in return she gave the much-needed nourishment for the whole family.

“Interpreters are always in demand in Malaya. English traders, the courts and police department are constantly in dire need of interpreters,” David persuaded.

“I am very much used to my life of teaching the children in school.”

“If you don’t like being an interpreter, reputed companies like Paterson & Simons would be more than happy to employ you in their office.”

“I shall certainly consider your idea, David.”

“Are you worried about the travel by ship beyond the pale?”

Ramasamy laughed, “Having seen only from far during my childhood the waves at Chendhur, I hardly know the sea.”

“Then you must be afraid of the quarantine.”

“I don’t know about that too. Please enlighten me.”

“Quarantine won’t be required if you can go as an independent migrant. I will refer you to my good friend Adam. He helps with alacrity.”

"I have absolutely no doubts on that."

"The amount you earn the whole year here, you will be able to send home every month."

"This man should be ostracized. Look at him entertaining the beef eater regularly in his house." The neighbor waylaid in officiously loud Tamil.

"Sambu, am I not alive and kicking? Why speak the words aimed at me to your walls? Come on in front of me and talk to me," Ramasamy said with a peal of authoritative laughter. The other side fell silent. David smiled.

"He was asking me if he could join us for a coffee. I said he's most welcome. Before I forget, is there any possibility of tracing my uncle? Could you find out any clues?"

"I have formally asked the person in charge in the department. Having promised to help, he says decades back; thousands were taken to Uganda, Kenya for railway jobs, to Trinidad to toil in sugar and coffee plantation and other industries."

"He was my father's only sibling. Born after fourteen years, he was very much doted at home. For some trivial reason he ran away from home to join a recruitment drive, they'd heard them from people."

"You have told me before, and I can very well empathize."

Meenakshi muttered, "I won't come with you anywhere," as she hurried inwards to the kitchen. Ramasamy was surprised by her voicing her opinion.

Later in the afternoon, her father came from his village. As he drank the filtered coffee, he tried to talk his son in law out of his travel plans. "It's said in the *sashtras*[8] that crossing the ocean,.."

8 *Sashtras* - Hindu scriptures

"Enough of your palaverings. I don't need anyone's opinion here. There is no turning back now. Your daughter is free to do as she pleases," Ramasamy put a full stop to the conversation.

Dear, I owe you an apology for not coming today. My dear grandsire is very sick back home. I got the telegram last night, and so I'm boarding the ship to London the day after tomorrow. I hope to see him recover and return by the time our little one is born. Always yours, D. 27th September1940, Friday.

II

Tall and stout Adam, with bright golden blond hair, had come to port Swettenham to receive him. "Ramasamy?" he looked deep into his eyes.

"Yes Sir," he extended his hand. Shaking it fondly he said, "Please call me Adam."

"Thank you. And I'm Rama."

"How well you fit David's description! Despite your fatigue, you smile so genially. Now I know why my quondam schoolmate cherishes his mentor."

Smiling weakly, Ramasamy looked down. "The tasteless gruel they'd served on board didn't suit my system. With the salty and sultry winds, my seasickness worsened. In the past few days, I drank just water."

"You will be fine in a day. There is a doctor in the same building."

After ambling a few steps together, Adam tried to take the trunk from his hand.

"Thank you. I should be able to manage."

"David has specifically elaborated on your staunch vegetarianism."

"I had brought with me some bananas and murukku that lasted but only for the first few days. Ramasamy said.

"One's food habit is like one's language, you learn them both and abide by from birth,"

"I can't agree more on that."

Most of the passengers alighting were brought to be employed as labourers in the plantations. They were sent to the quarantine camp. Their clothes were infested, and they are vaccinated upon entering. If it does not take effect, they are vaccinated again on the eighth day. Upon discharge, they are shifted to depots.

Officers were bribed one rupee per head by the *kanganis*[9]. Otherwise, for every twenty labourers they sometimes get fifty rupees. The money spent was deducted from the labourers' wages over a period.

"It's not easy to find out about the stealthy bribery."

"That's one of the depots where labourers are collected by kanganis," Adam pointed.

A youth of about twenty argued boldly, "*Naa vara maatten. Ganesan kangani varuvaaru* [10]."

"Admirably strong-minded lad, I see in him a future kangani !" laughed Adam. Ramasany looked at everything with fresh wondering eyes.

"Unwell labourers are sometimes forced by the kanganis to work because he gets two cents per head every day as commission. Strait's government officers of Negapatnam, Avadi warn the kanganis on these practices, but they continue secretly like nothing ever happened," Adam explained. "I wanted to ask you the meaning of the word 'absquatulate'"

---

9 *Kanganis* - supervisors

10 *naa vara maaten. Ganesan kangani varuvaaru* - (in Tamil) I won't come. Ganesan kangani will come.

"Depart or to leave abruptly."

"How spontaneous! Thank you."

"..."

"How many children do you have, Rama?"

"Four. All four are in elementary school."

With the lingering fears of the Japanese invasion at any time, the affairs of the estates were more disorganised than ever, and the Malayan government had to nip unionism in the bud smartly. There were absolutely no chances for it to sprout ever again.

"Too many mouths to feed, hardly any income, and so children die of malnutrition in India, I hear."

"True. The great famine, overpopulation, and poverty are becoming synonymous to Indian society," Ramasamy tried to engage in the conversation.

"The recent initial statistics show India alone has had thirty big famines in the last century, and about thirty-two million lives lost."

"Unfortunately so, and I won't be surprised if the number is larger."

"Have you seen David's sweetheart?" He asked beaming broadly as they walked through the busy street.

"I didn't know he had one," Ramasamy said with a shy smile and a blush.

"Neither did I know until recently when he opened up to me. I don't know who it is."

"*Beralih, Beri cara*[11]," a trishaw puller shouted as he weaved through.

Workers had stopped going to work for the past month at a stretch demanding higher wages, proper medical facilities, education for children and better living conditions. In their dhotis, with bare torsos, the men

11 *Beralih, Beri cara* – Move, move, give way. - in Malay

looked worn out and tired. Women were wrapped clumsily in their saris and head cloth and had their small bundles tugged under their arms.

"Their indecorous habiliments are intriguing," he said a little hesitantly. Ramasamy was bewildered by the different races around in the busy streets. The roadside shops and hawkers seemed to challenge his sense of smell, he observed.

Adam said as he boarded the car. "Their demands are not at all unreasonable." Ramasamy sat beside him.

"Like any other community, theirs is also evolving," explained Adam. Earning fifty cents a day, the labourers were under constant vigilance. Life was tough. Each estate had a *samy veedu*[12]. Their dwelling places were attap houses with mud walls. About ten square feet accommodated six persons or sometimes two or three couples. Privacy was an issue in their initial stage, and slowly they became blind to. Only some larger estates sold rice at cost, milk provided free for children of the coolies, and crèches were funded, for their children.

After placing the travel trunk in the boot, driver Cheng said as he took the wheels. "The labour unrest is escalating, these days, Sir."

"Yes, I have been following. And to think they have been at it for almost eight years now. Decades have passed since the rubber has crept in and yet the estate issues continue to remain unresolved."

"This time they are demanding the release of their leaders, Sir," said Cheng.

"Oh yes! That reminds me, one of them is self-respect group from Madras, I hear. Rama might know."

"No, I don't know of any such people," Ramasamy said politely.

"They want to close all the toddy shops in the estates. They wish to fight for remaining mounted on their bicycles in front of the English when they happen to pass by," Cheng said as he drove past busy streets.

12 *Samy veedu* - an alter / place of worship - in Tamil

"Imagine expecting wages on par with the Chinese workers! These people detest those who come from Ceylon. Not just that, they dislike those coming from Travancore as well," Adam said as he looked at Ramasamy.

"Please rest well in the room. I will come tomorrow. I will tell the doctor downstairs to visit you, maybe in an hour." He nodded looking politely at him. "Rama, we leave this weekend to Singapore."

Dear, I was very happily thrilled when you said yesterday that the baby growing in you is mine. None would have any idea. I am waiting to take you both to England, introduce to all my people and formally marry you. We will flee if that is required because I doubt your family would approve. Yours, D. 18th March 1940, Monday.

III

Adam and Ramasamy boarded the train to Singapore. As they settled down in their seats, Adam started talking. "The island is full of mangrove swamps, with a population of less than a million, rubber failed miserably. With the help of the Chinese secret society, only opium houses and brothels have been flourishing. Sin-galore," Adam laughed. "You would start loving this place so much that you might not like to leave."

Ramasamy listened as he looked out the window now and then. It was shining with a smell of freshness after a torrential downpour. He was worried if his bunch of bananas and the packet peanuts could last him till he could think of any facilities to cook his meal that night.

"Straits Settlements Legal Service is being formed. Local services office is where you will work, Rama. You will be one of the first few Indians to work there. My workplace is just a few building away. There shouldn't be any problem for you in the office. Should they affront you, please let me know. I will immediately intervene."

As the night fell, after alighting, they walked out of the Bukit Tanjong Pagar station. "I have my car parked here," Adam said. He drove his car in Bukit Timah Road when he asked puckishly, "Can you cook your meals?"

Ramasamy gave a dissenting shake of the head, yes. He was stupefied entirely by dishabille women on the streets. The humidity was striking, he thought.

"Your meals will be arranged with another similar family very soon."

"Appreciate your good efforts to help me in this foreign land."

Ramasamy walked after Adam. When they climbed up a flight of stairs, they could hear a few men talking in Tamil. "Netaji, who was under house arrest, slipped out disguised as a Muslim insurance agent. Everyone including the guards was fast asleep. Looks like he first went to Berari near Dhanbad. From there he went to Delhi by train, and there he took the Frontier mail to Peshawar. Upon reaching Kabul, he sought help in the Russian consulate, they say."

"The people in Calcutta came to know of the 'Great escape' only after ten days. What a tight slap on the face of British Intelligence!"

"Hush!" they said on seeing Adam.

It was a decent room, which Ramasamy would share with a young accountant.

"Stay in this shophouse for a few days. Very soon, I shall look for proper accommodation for you." Ramasamy nodded.

Adam left him in the temporary lodging.

The loquacious group continued their political chattering from where they had left. "With the new passport made in an Italian name,

Bose had escaped to Germany, then to Moscow to recruit for INA. In Azad Hind Radio, created by him, he made in his first speech. "I am Subash Chandra Bose who is still alive and talking to you," brought shock waves to those who thought him to be a formidable foe of the British rule in India."

"He referred to Gandhi as 'the father of the nation.' Didn't he?"

"Yes, of course, I heard. I think Bose is an outstanding leader of not just a nation or two but of the whole continent of Asia."

Ramasamy just smiled as he removed his overcoat to lie down to rest. He continued to listen as he placed his things on a table.

They looked at him. "Do you speak Tamil or Telugu? Feel at home," They started talking to him in Tamil.

"Don't worry. Malaya will not let you down. We've all been working here for a few years, mostly to keep books for traders and shop owners. Singapore is a land of opportunities."

"Uprooted there, not yet enrooted here but we're still alive. So we continue to remain here."

"We came not expecting any better conditions than just to be alive."

"My Chinese friend Liang often recites, 'Bury me facing northwest so I lay facing my land' like a poem in Chinese."

"I have a big family in Nagapattinam. I visit them."

"Yes, and a small family here," they laughed loudly slapping each other's back.

Ramasamy gave rapt expression as he listened to their honest sharing.

"We plan to go to the temple. But will you pray to Muneeswaran? He is mighty. He can grant your wish."

"You will like it here, Iyer."

"Here, Indian labourers involved in road building, building constructions have their own dwelling dormitories."

"But Chinese migrants were mostly hawkers, vendors, merchants. Chinese coolies starve and slept on rocky roadsides to save every cent to send money home."

Ramasamy missed his family, his school, his students, his lessons, his chair, his books, and everything. He wrote to them often. His brother replied to most of his letters. The letter carrying the news of Neela's death devastated him.

"By the time you reach, everything would have been done and over. Things would be settling down. If you send them the money it might be more useful to them," Adam convinced Ramasamy.

With choking throat, he said, "She turns twenty only next month. I refused all the meaningless rituals that are in practice thrust upon a widow in our community. Except for the few months in her husband's house, she was all along with us. I brought her up like my own daughter. She was naturally strong in the English language. I just can't accept that Neela is no more," head bent down as he shed large tears. Adam pressed his shaking shoulders.

"*Lai lai, wonton lai.*"[13] When Ramsamy heard someone down on the road shouting, he looked at their faces.

"Oh, that's the Chinese hawker selling hot wonton soup."

The months that followed not just brought in money but also a lot of acquaintances and friends. Ramasamy slowly felt that he was settling down. He was getting to know the intricate problems that the immigrants brought along and all the problems they faced here.

---

13 *Lai lai, wonton lai – Come on, come and have wonton! (Wonton - small dumplings or rolls with a savory filling, often of minced pork, usually eaten boiled in a soup.)* A vendor calling out his customers, in Chinese.

Adam entered the room, “I heard you have not been turning up for work. They said you have fallen ill.”

When Ramasamy tried to rise from his bed, Adam stopped him. “Goodness gracious! You have lost weight beyond recognition.”

“It is indeed surprising how these locals survive the remittent and intermittent fevers. And they mostly go for the traditional medicines.” Rama managed to force a slight wavering smile as he spoke.

Adam laughed, “Looks like the Mosquitoes have the guts to avenge only the migrants like us.”

“Adam, if you could please arrange for me to go back to my family, I shall be indebted to you forever,” Ramasamy pleaded feebly.

“It’s undisputedly inopportune, but you will recover, Rama.”

“The Chinese concoction is also not helping the Malaria.”

“Be it what it may we shall plan your departure after you recover, I promise. You need the energy to endure at least the return journey.”

“Erudite that I have always remained, David and you created for me to acquire a rich exposure that I would cherish all my life. Though only for a year, I appreciate this opportunity”

Ramasamy waited patiently for over a month as he recovered.

Dear, Needless to say, I was astonished to hear that your husband died in cholera. Your marriage was arranged too hurriedly, my intuitions told me. Will you try to meet me at dawn when you go to fetch water in the river? It’s more than a year since we talked. I have so much to share. Look forward to seeing you. Yours, D. 13th January 1940, Saturday.

IV

With the cool November breeze brushing his face, Ramasamy reached the entrance of his house. The nadir came when he set his eyes on the blue grey-eyed toddler with dark brown soft bristles on his head, he froze stunned. The trunk in his hand fell on the ground with a loud metallic sound.

The one-year-old little boy went behind Meenakshi upon seeing him. "Go, go to your *mama*[14]," she tried to pull him gently from behind. "The children are away in school. They wanted to stay home when you arrive." She was trying to say something to ease the fury building up in her husband.

Ramasamy glared at his brother who stammered, "*Anna*[15], we wanted to tell you before your return but,..."

"When you could easily write about her demise, couldn't you write about this?" He pointed his finger at the child. "Make sure this anathema never appears in front of me."

Leaving his footwear outside, he went straight to his study. After sitting there for a few minutes, he shouted loud and clear in Tamil, "I refuse to speak or use English from this moment." Everyone at home was terrified to hear his rumbling declaration.

"Calm down Rama. The loss is not yours. Don't do anything in anger," Sambu shouted from his premises. But before he could run over to stop him, Ramasamy pulled out in an intense fury the dictionary that he treasured so dear like his own life, removed the loose-fitting black coat that he always wore and took them both hurriedly to the back yard.

Sambu froze upon seeing him fling them sideways into the stinging spread out furious flame that boiled water in a cauldron that sat on top.

---

14 *Mama-* maternal uncle - in Tamil

15 *Anna* - Elder brother

Ramasamy, the free dictionary became silent, a painful silence created a bitterness in the house. He knew if he opened his mouth his tongue would only spill all elite English. Reclining on his chair, with his upper cloth and without the turban and the shirt, he ruminated all day. He went in to eat during his meal times.

One day when Sambu casually approached him, "What's meaning of the word misanthrope?" Ramasamy almost opened his mouth, "A per,.., " shut his mouth up. Sambu held a piece of paper in which he wrote the meaning - a person who hates or distrusts humankind.

It was the new moon day in the month of the scorching April. After having finished all the morning rituals of offerings to the ancestors followed by meals, Ramasamy relaxed reclining in his armchair. He did not open his mouth when he heard Sambu's innocuous chiding, "Having crossed the sea, why do you even bother with these rituals, Rama? What's the point?"

With her calf at her side, Lakshmi went on mooing. "Maaah,.." After hearing Rama say, "Varen ma," she was quiet for hardly a few minutes. Later, she restarted her calling.

With a slight pride and a minor proud sulk, he got up to head towards the kitchen. There was a large twenty-liter brass drum three-fourth full of draff mixed with all perishable like vegetable peels and wastes along with the collected water used to cleanse rice and pulses before cooking. Lakshmi loved that.

"Wait a minute, Lakshmi. I am bringing it," he said lovingly in Tamil as if talking to his own daughter.

As he lifted it, there was a dislocating sound at his lower spine. He fell straight on his back leaving hold of the big vessel more than half full of swill. The fall was so forceful that his badly injured head bled profusely. Below his head on the uneven cemented floor formed a large round red patch that widened fast like a blotting paper absorbing ink. His eyes froze as if staring at the ceiling.

Meenakshi rushed running and started lamenting. Seeing him motionless in a pool of blood, she swooned.

The funeral saw more people than expected. Relatives, friends, teachers, students, past students from far and near came to pay respects. Many were in tears.

As was the norm, women were out of sight in rooms. "Hiding certain things is beyond us humans." After sharing all the news about Neela, the women's utterances came to the laid out corpse. "He is not even thirty-five, you know," said a lady glibly.

"My grandfather used to say that there is no salvation for a Brahmin who crosses the ocean. That should have turned out to be his bad luck. All things look so much preordained," said another morbidly in a hushed voice. "Recently he was unusually quiet and peevish," said Sambu's wife. "One could easily smell the rat."

None was concerned about the devastated Meenakshi who lay at one corner of the dark room with her head on her mother's lap. An elderly widow went on rambling, "Just like they stripped me of my jewels, flowers, bangles, hair, and ornaments, in another two weeks, Meenakshi will also cover her shaven head with her beige cotton sari and leave in a bullock cart to her eldest brother's care in Aruppokkottai. What else can a woman do?" When someone voiced, "Times are changing," she said sternly, "Not everyone has a brother like Neela. I was much younger but had no children. Meenakshi will have four young ones towing." She wiped her eyes with her sari edge.

Along with her calf, Lakshmi was sold off.

"He could only buy some farmlands within a year. But, with all the earned rectitude gone he was inward." Men at the pyol casually moved their conversation on to politics. "Luckily, he left that place months before the Japs occupied."

"Exactly my sentiments! Churchill considers the defeat at Singapore as one of the most humiliatingly worst British defeats of all time," Sambu's friend said in lower volume. "Gandhi is objecting to his attempts on the vivisection of India."

The Morris that halted attracted everyone's attention. Everyone including ladies was curious to take a peep through tiny windows and door gaps.

"Having lost my grandfather three months back, I could come back to India only last week," David said to Ramasamy's brother as he entered with his slightly bent physique. "Please accept my condolences. The loss is beyond words."

The brother gave an inimical, cold, contemptuous stare. Suddenly, he became a little restless, but no one talked.

Feeling awkward, David stood at one corner looking at the people around. "Can I please take with me one of his dictionaries as his remembrance? He was my best friend, guide and philosopher."

"Take this with you instead," said the angry brother vehemently as he bent forward to pull the child from the nearby room. All those present watched awestruck. David looked up at the window pane. "Neela?"

"She died minutes after giving birth." With teary eyes and distorted face, David walked towards the child who clung tight to his uncle. David lifted the child whose nose reminded him of Neela. Holding him close to his chest David said, "Please kindly look after him another few days. I shall certainly come back for my son," and put the child down slowly. After looking around, David squatted down to kiss him once before departing hurriedly.

***

The Peasant Girl

Momo held out her thin porcelain smooth arms to show her swollen red wrists. In a low, sad voice with welled up eyes she bewailed, "Only once I can use the washing machine, they insist. Most of the other clothes I must only wash by hand." Her employer's siblings and their families stayed in walkable distances. About eight children of various ages and eleven adults came over to dump their laundry daily and to have their meals. "Before I started work, they said there are only two adults and two children in the family."

"Does your agent know all this?"

"I don't know if she understands whatever I tell her. They always come one by one or in pairs, and I can't cook at one go but only the required quantity upon seeing them, like in a restaurant. Last month, I forgot to wash one t-shirt, and they cut ten dollars from my salary. I have to work fast, but I can't go to sleep without showering, they compel. When I am showering, they will ask me to come out fast because the water bill will go up. I'm woken up very early in the morning."

Petite that she was, she certainly looked drained compared to the bright, naive and fresh-faced she had arrived months back, Bina remembered. Clipping her laundry on the portable hanger in the common corridor, Momo paused to look beyond to view the wall hanging in Bina's living room.

"Oh, that's *Ganpati Bappa*[16]*,*" Bina said.

"In our culture, the King of Brahmas is called Arsi. He lost in a war with Śakra, the King of Devas. As mutually agreed, a head of an elephant was placed onto Arsi's body with a severed head which later became our Ganesha."

"What an interesting variation!"

With various intricate facial expressions Momo continued, "Arsi was so powerful that if the head were to be thrown into the sea, it would dry up immediately if thrown onto land it would scorch dry, and if thrown up into the sky, it would turn into fury flames. So, Sakra ordained the head to be carried by one princess devi after another, taking turns for a year each."

Momo suddenly switched to her problems, "My father says, stay for two years, we must pay off the debts. But it is tough here. This madam is very fierce." Though aware of the pugnacity of the lady next door, Bina could not respond to that except to carefully say, "Try some other agent for a change of employer."

"I don't know any. Can you please help?"

Later in the day, Bina browzed the net to find the contact details of many agents. "I don't know *lah* if calling them can help but no harm in trying."

"Please help me post these two letters." Except 'Myanmar' everything else was written in curves like some charming classic motifs.

16 *Ganpati Bappa* – The elephant faced Hindu deity.

"This one is for my family, and the other is for Zaw," Momo said shyly. Bina took them refusing the two dollars she tried to give for the postage.

***

Though the locals very easily switched to Myanmar, English speakers preferred to call it Burma to mean 'Be upstairs ready my angel,' Momo said. The idea of calling Myanmar meant to be a little softer on the military regime, faded soon. About eleven kilometers from the town of Putao, her village stood serenely with scattered houses. The three-wheeled tuk-tuks helped the villagers commute to the city. The thatched huts made out of bamboo sheaths and wood were surrounded by lush paddy, corn and vegetable fields. Some households had a large bamboo chute that transported water from the creeks up above the green mountains, beyond which stood the ice-capped lower eastern Himalayan range vaguely visible in contrast to the clear blue sky.

As the eldest child in the family, Momo used to manage mainly, the two buffaloes, a dozen chickens, and all the household chores. After dropping out of high school, she started helping her parents in their patch of land tilling, sowing, weeding, watering and harvesting.

"Momo, don't forget to include *Thanaka* when you are packing. Singapore is hot, they say," her mother had reminded. Believed to remove acne the yellowish paste of a perennial tree bark ground on a slate slab, has a fragrance similar to sandalwood. Since childhood, she has always applied it on her cheeks, the bridge of her nose, fingers.

The day she was sent with her maternal uncle to Yangon to board the flight to Singapore, Zaw had planned to meet her in the outskirts of the village. They ambled along the small common pond with floating lilies and leaves among the dry and rotten twigs and roots. The cool morning breeze carried the fragrance of the blooms. "They may be the descendants of a family that owned two elephants to serve the British timber traders those days. But all those were in the past. Not even the slightest trace of their honour is left now. Singapore is a good country. *Garuhcite hkyinnnhaint kaunggsaw hpyit* [17]," her uncle repeated all that her father had said many times.

She was in hand-loomed navy blue longyi and plain but frilled sky blue blouse. Upon seeing her uncle from afar, Zaw spontaneously pulled the large bamboo hat down to cover his face, as he cycled away without stopping, but in a flash thrust a letter in her hand.

My dearest Momo, it started and had all his usual romantic out pours that also touched on how he would miss her and contained the essence of '*I will be in Singapore at the earliest. I'm prepared to work as a construction worker*'. Momo kept safe the letter preciously in her purse. Although she knew pretty well that he was only dreaming of the impossible, his words certainly made her happy.

Momo was washing the Honda Mobilio, the six-seater and the Nissan Sylphy. Placed in between to dry in the Sun were the Chicco Bravo Stroller and the baby seat that was already washed. As if waiting to see Bina, she smiled. "Can I talk with you?" Halting instantly, Bina looked at her.

"My father called last week on this landline from town. The debtors are pressurizing him. I'm keeping with me my three months' salary. They don't want to help me send the money."

"Why?"

"Last night she said go tomorrow. But with so many chores to complete, today morning she said I can't go."

"It is their responsibility to help you send the money."

"She says she is too busy. She has no time."

"..."

17 *Garuhcite hkyinnnhaint kaunggsaw hpyit* - Be careful and be good

"One of my brothers stopped schooling to help my father in the land. I am unfortunate. I want to go back to my village." Her face looked more like a ten-year-old rather than a twenty-two year old. "Mam scolded and scolded till midnight. She thinks I am always talking on the landline when I am alone. I don't know anyone here. Sir said, 'Come on *lah*, you have a daughter too, why do you keep scolding her?' Mam fought back more fiercely with him. '*Nee shou shamma?* Don't curse my baby, okay? Aren't you ashamed, isn't she also your daughter?' I ran away to the kitchen," Momo looked as if she was about to cry.

Suddenly, she digressed to ask plaintively, "Madam, can you please help?"

"Help?"

"To send my money home."

"But.."

"Please, ma'am. I'm scared to go out. I want to remit the money fast to my family." She gave the thousand dollars.

"I must ask my husband first."

***

In the evening, Anil raised several questions. "*Kyun is bekar kaam me padthi ho Bina*? And how do you know if that's her money? What if her employer does not like us helping her? Their domestic helpers may come and go every few months, but they are always our neighbour. Though not too friendly, we cannot afford to antagonize them."

"Just this once, the poor thing is pleading with me."

"If it is her salary, why is she so scared to ask them to help?" Anil asked as he left for office.

Bina took the piece of paper in which Momo had written the peninsular plaza address and her mother's account number. When she was wearing her sandals, Momo looked through the gate said, "You, please take a cab, mam."

"I can go by train. No worries, I can afford the time."

"Whether you take the cab or not, you please take 50 dollars for yourself, and send only 900 to my family."

Bina laughed at that. "No, no. I will send the whole amount."

"All banks are closed in our country for the next two weeks."

"Two weeks?"

"Ya, the new year is coming," She beamed. "Our's is in mid-April."

"Songkran?"

"In other Theravada Buddhist countries like Thailand and Laos, they call it Sokran. For us it is Thingyan."

Thingyan, she explained, is celebrated toward the end of the hot and dry season lasted three to five days. Standing on the small temporary bamboo stages erected along the streets, people splashed water on the passersby. Powerful water pipes douse people driving by in bikes, jeeps, and trucks. Children used water pistols to drench their friends, relatives, and anyone else in range. Only monks and the elderly are left undisturbed. The water symbolized the washing away of the previous year's bad luck and sins. Captive fish and birds were released as an act of merit, and special feasts were held for monks.

"Our new year signifies Brahma's head changing hands," she concluded with an innocent natural smile.

***

At the peninsular plaza, the golden crown shop was closed. There was a phone number stuck outside on the wavy tin shutter door. Whether to wait or to go, Bina wondered for a few minutes. "If I go back, when can I come again?" she thought. Bina asked in the nearby beauty parlor whose owner said the shop usually opens by eleven. She decided to wait outside the shop, looking around.

The shop owner, a friendly lady in her forties, came. Greeting with a smile and a nod, she opened the shop and offered Bina a seat. Before she could talk, the telephone rang. The lady smiled twice at Bina politely but went on jabbering in Burmese. After having finished with the call, she took the paper with the details, "Sorry about that. Oh, this girl had called me yesterday! She said an Indian lady would come."

"So, you know her."

"I have never seen her. Even her friend also doesn't come here these days. I thought this girl started sending money through someone else because for the past two or three months she never sent money through us."

"This looks like a sundry shop, do you really transfer money?"

"The next door shop money transfer service is my friend's. I collect on her behalf when she comes late."

"Do you give a receipt?"

"Of course, we do. Don't worry."

"I don't know how the helper trusts me so much."

"Because you are pretty," she said wide-eyed in an attempt to please.

"You mean good looking people are all trustworthy?"

"No, no. I didn't mean that, haha,.."

***

Zaw's was the wooden house that had a storey above and the only big house of its kind in the village. He was the youngest of the three sons. When he was past his teenage, his eldest brother, about ten years older, was getting married to a girl from the next village. The astrologer had given a date in May which was just a fortnight away. Arrangements went on full swing.

Festoons and simple decorations brought about a significant change to the surrounding. Women were clad in their traditional best. A few of them had a single large flower adorning behind the ear, inserted at the base of their elegant chignons.

Two monks, clad in rich maroon robes, had been invited to bless the couple and recite the protective *paritta*[18]. Almsgiving feast was organised in the morning. Several dishes of vegetables were cooked and displayed along with rice on a small table. As if it were a single giant dish, the table was carefully and respectfully lifted by the members of the family including the couple. One of the monks just touched the table to signify his acceptance. There was laughter around when the other monk gestured to receive it from him. Subsequently, everyone with joined palms in reverence, witnessed the two monks eating. Momo could only get glimpses of the event.

Momo suppressed her laughter when she thought they were all watching the monks like the feeding time at the zoo.

Suddenly she caught Zaw intently looking at her. With a smile, she gestured him to observe the ritual.

Later, a Brahmin, the master of ceremonies who was hired by the town began the wedding by blowing the conch shell. He joined the palms of the couple, wrapping them in white cloth, dipped in a silver bowl. The bride and groom were seated on cushions next to each other. Their palms remained joined together. After chanting a few Sanskrit mantras,

18 *Paritta* - the Buddhist practice of reciting certain verses from scriptures in order to ward off ill luck or dangerous conditions.

the Brahmin took the couple's joined palms out of the bowl and blew the conch shell once again to end the ceremony. After the village entertainers' simple traditional songs, the wedding ended with a short speech by the head of the village.

During the feast, the couple ate from the same plate. That's when the ambiance suddenly turned astir. The police came to arrest Zaw's father's younger brother, who at the top of his voice shouted at the officials, "Why don't you arrest all the two million farmers cultivating opium in more than half a million hectares. Why arrest only me? As if only I do it."

Zaw's uncle in the next village had farming tractors, two healthy horses that pulled large cart and herds of pigs and several well-yielding cows. He seldom visited their town. When he did, he used to go into the wilds up the hills during the dry months to hunt for meat and also to pluck some herbs, which were his hobbies.

After that incident, Zaw's family was affected both financially and otherwise. Momo was not allowed to see Zaw or meet him. "You can choose anyone else but him," her parents kept insisting.

There were minor tiffs between the two families because Zaw would not stop looking for opportunities to meet her. That's when her parents decided to send her away to Singapore to work as a domestic helper. For a year, every day she visited the town with an escort most of the time, to complete a crash course on spoken English.

***

When Bina walked past their house, Momo looked through the window, pulling the curtain aside. The common corridor was wet after the flash rains. Gesturing thumps up, she showed the receipt to Momo, she joined her palms in gratitude and hurried in moving her lips 'later.'

Next day morning, when Bina gave her the receipt, "So, I owe you 5 dollars?" Momo asked.

"No *lah.* I sent only 995 after the five dollars towards the remittance."

"Thanks."

"Next time, I cannot help you, ok? Please don't ask me."

"I won't ask. Which brand tea do you use, madam?"

"Why?"

"What is your brand name?" Momo smiled hesitantly.

"My brand is from India."

"Can I get it in ntuc supermarket?"

"No."

"I thought of buying for you." After a few seconds, "I want to go back home," she started crying.

"You will be happy with your family." Bina tried to sound neutral.

"Mam called my agent and shouted. She wants me to stay." Remembering Anil's warnings, Bina managed to remain unaffected. Hearing the family exiting the lift, Momo, face full of fear, impetuously rushed back inside the house. Bina greete with a courteous smile, the sisters who arrived grandly with their Charlotte Olympia, Valentino, Kipling, and Vera Bradley.

***

In the wee hours that night, there was a loud commotion next door that woke Bina up. She got up to drink water. Before going back to bed, she looked through the peephole. Their living room window was not shut fully.

With vehemence, the lady of the house shouted, "She always says want to go home, want to go home. You know, she had a long list of agents. I don't know where she got them. She is not as innocent as she seems. It's best to send her back." Her husband said nothing and yet she said, "You don't interfere, okay? Momo, come and open your bags right away. I need to check before you repack. We have more than enough time for your boarding."

***

Feeling a little guilty, Bina described everything to Anil at the breakfast table as he was getting ready to leave for work. "It might be a blessing in disguise for the girl but may not be for her family back home. But it's certainly a lesson for you." She could not but agree with his words.

After Anil had left for work, Bina caught up with some sleep and woke up suddenly upon hearing someone knock hard on the neighbour's door. After ignoring it for a few minutes, she got up and went to the door to look through the peephole.

With unkempt hair and a tired, tanned face and a confused expression, medium height and build man with baggage and luggage with the Air Asia airline tag, stood there in front of the next door. He looked about twenty-five.

Opening the door, through the locked gate, Bina asked, "I don't think anyone is inside the house. Are you looking for someone?" Not looking into her eyes for more than a second, he turned his gaze down to the floor. "Momo," he said hesitantly.

"Zaw?"

***

Beyond borders

With moist and dismayed eyes, a foreign worker, in clothes mildly smeared with grease and paint, stood first in the growing queue. Pusillanimously lost in thought, and he looked like a Bangladeshi, Anu guessed.

Just behind the Bangladeshi, a middle-aged rotund Chinese man was leaning on the side rails with two sizeable red plastic shopping bags placed near his feet. Oblivious to the surrounding, he was busy talking on his mobile, thanking and laughing with exaggerated courtesy, "*Hǎi méiyǒu, xièxiè.*"

The moment Anu saw her son's eyes sparkling brighter, she knew the reason, and she'd guessed it right. Crawling on one of the large plastic bags carried by a Chinese man was a huge fly that caught the keen attention of ten-year-old Kani. He couldn't take his eyes off.

As always she was fascinated by his interest displayed even before he had turned one. From as early as seven months he used to look for tiny ants and insects in the corners of the marble floor and follow them crawling on fours. Though rare, they would never fail to catch his attention. And flying insects thrilled him all the more. Long before he could say the word, "*Amma*," to call her, he had learned to say '*Poochchi*[19]', in Tamil, which made history, becoming the first word he learned to speak.

Eager to continue where they had left their conversation just before leaving home, Anu asked her husband, "And what did that Pinoy colleague of yours exactly say to anger you that much? Somu, you didn't tell me the details."

Excited, wide-eyed Somu said, "He had the cheek to say right on my face that without them our country will cease to function. Can you believe that, Anu?"

Although the haze due to the conflagration in the Sumatran forests seemed to have reduced to healthy levels, about six or seven out of the ten migrant faces wore the N9 masks.

"He means, without the Filipinos?"

"I am sure he must have meant all foreign workers in general, I suppose. I couldn't stand his temerity, you know. Seething through, I was intensely searing inside." She just nodded looking at his face.

His cute chubby face was becoming more and more rounded with the receding hairline, she thought. The black curls highlighted his already fair complexion.

As if muttering to herself Anu said, "Humans seem to push the days of the week just for their weekend, when they live." The queues were suddenly getting longer, Anu observed.

The bus interchange was filling with an erratic mixture of children shrieking, loud laughter of young people in groups, buses maneuvering and halting, bus doors opening and closing.

19 *Poochchi* - A generic term to refer to any kind of insect.

Mandarin, Tamil, Malay, Tagalog, Hokkien, and Bangla heard here and there were certainly not mellifluous, but an intriguing babel. The aroma of the satay from the nearby hawker wafted along with the breeze.

The breeze bore the message of the approaching showers. The slowly gathering dark clouds not just dimmed the sunlight but had suddenly increased the humidity.

Being one of the first few in the line for the route number 960, getting seats of their choice was not difficult.

The Bangladeshi worker walked straight to the back and took the left window seat of the long row of last seats.

Keeping his sight on the fly, Kani slowly walked ahead but slowly.

"He went on saying things like they are a cheerful and contented bunch even with lower wages."

"Lower?" Anu asked with an intrigued expression.

"Ya lah. Their wages are somewhat lower than us locals."

"True," she agreed.

The stout Chinese man placed the bags purposely on the adjacent seat so that the foreign workers boarding behind wouldn't be able to occupy the seat near him.

Watching the fly, Kani stood there blocking the way for the other passengers. Anu hurriedly pulled him along. "Isn't it a common house fly, just a little larger?" Somu hushed. They moved to the rear. Kani's focus remained on the fly as he reluctantly walked turning his head backward. "No."

As the bus exited at the Woodlands interchange, Somu continued, "You know Anu, I couldn't help telling him, why you don't go back since you get paid low here. But he left the place abruptly without saying more when he went on to say I must learn to be happy."

"You?"

"He meant us, Singaporeans," Somu said lowering his voice.

Near the exit, seated at the center of the bus the three domestic workers dressed in their weekend best, dolled up in all accessories, started watching videos happily, ready to enjoy their off day. One of them answered a call, "*One ang paraan, sanay maging late*," assuring their punctuality to the friends on the other side.

Seated right behind his parents, next to the Bangladeshi worker, Kani kept getting up restlessly from his seat to look at the fly.

When a plump middle-aged Malay woman boarded at the Marsiling station, one of the foreign worker seated behind the driver spontaneously got up to give her the seat. The lady hesitated for a second and was about to lumber to the back when the other guy at the window seat followed suit. Happily, she sat on the aisle seat keeping all her bags and belonging on the window seat before she started looking out of the window.

Taking a look around within the bus, Anu said, "It's fine Somu. Not like you had feared. I can even see a few empty seats."

"You don't know, darling. This bus really gets crowded on Sundays. We could have gone shopping next weekend after our car is back from servicing," he sulked.

"Oh come on, Somu. Look at him! He seems to be enjoying the bus ride."

"If not for the parking woes in Little India area, I wouldn't choose to travel in this bus, especially during the weekend," he sulked for the third time.

When the fly flew to the rear, it landed on the tab the domestic worker was holding. She jumped and shooed it off with a loud giggle. Her two friends joined in the amusement.

Kani got excited and shrieked, "Pa, look he is flying this way!" Suddenly feeling shy for having expressed loudly, he sat on his seat quietly observing.

The insect had comfortably settled on the glass window near the exit. Fixing his gaze on the fly, Kani sat calmly, glancing at other things once in a while. He shared his discovery, "Musca domestica," tugging at his mother's shoulder from the back of her seat. He pointed to the fly when Anu turned from the front seat to smile at him.

After the first few stops, at the Kranji station, foreign workers were boarding in groups.

Somu gave her a, "I told you!" kind of a look.

"Kani needs to see some real world at least once in a while," Anu smiled gathering the locks of hair and tugging them behind her ears with her right hand.

There was an empty seat after the exit. A tall and slender looking Chinese woman who had boarded looked around, waved her hand with a pointed finger, "Go and sit there lah." The construction appeared to be a Tamil guy got up like an obedient student and moved to the back. With a haughty expression, "Thank you," she said curtly, almost half-heartedly.

"What do you mean Anu? Don't tell me that only crowded bus rides are real life," Somu chided with a laugh.

"Not exactly, but in a way yes," Anu beamed.

Many were startled when the Malay woman, in her attempt to alight at the Bukit Panjang CC advanced to the back saying, "Cannot taahan this anymore. Why are these people so smelly?» Right after getting off the bus, she threw an angry expression at the bus from where she stood.

"Ma, why is that old aunty rankling for no apparent reason?"

"Hush, hush, no. Are you bored? Want my mobile?"

"No," he said and went back to watch the big fly.

As the bus entered the BKE, most of them were getting busy texting. Most of them had dozed off in their seats. The bus suddenly quietened.

The two high housing board block of flats followed by a few private condominiums beyond the green wilds, on the right disappeared within minutes.

The long terrain ride with the lush natural habitat on either side of the expressway, as always brought a serene feeling within, Anu thought.

"Oh my God! I took the wrong set of shopping bags! I never bought these live crabs," the Chinese man suddenly jolted. He held the tied bag with a large partially visible creepy crab within.

He stood up to go near the driver. "You have to get off at the Tanglin CC and cross the road via the overhead bridge and board a bus back to Bukit Panjang," as he said calmly, the driver smartly kept his eyes on the road.

Kani was eager to have a look at the crab from near, but Somu said, "No need to go all the way there. We are speeding in the expressway Kani. It's enough to look from here. I thought you were scared of crabs," he chuckled.

"Of course, I wouldn't dare touch it, pa. Thought of a closer look. The crab looks unique," Kani said but sat back in his seat.

The Bangladeshi worker was sincerely trying hard to look away from the young Anglo Chinese couple in secret and mild canoodle at the right end of the long back seat. He had been talking seriously to someone for more than ten minutes. Sensing the network was bound to go erratic in the PIE, he winded up his conversation smartly, "*Jaanish. Achchaa, thaarpor kotha bolbo, han*?"

The road widening works near the exit to Eng Neo Avenue and Adams Road suddenly reminded of the city life.

"You look ravishing in this sari," Somu whispered in Anu's ear.

"And you have said that umpteen times, Somu. I still can't forget the day you stood at the shop dead against me choosing this." Reminiscing, they both laughed together and turned to look behind at Kani.

Very much familiar with the expressway, traffic, the downtown line works along the Bukit Timah road, Kani was observing all that he could, mostly within the bus as if he might never a get another chance to travel by bus.

Once at Whitley Road, the louring, urban face of the city showed. "This comes under the suborder Cyclorrhapha," Kani bent down to whisper into Somu's ears. The father forced a smile and looked at the fly.

Grumblingly, the Chinese man holding the large shopping bags alighted.

With not many passengers boarding or alighting, the bus streamlined through the Bukit Timah Road.

When the bus reached Little India, most of the commuters alighted. "Bus ride was damn interesting, Pa," Kani mused as he got down. Though sunny, the roads glittered wetly. The rains had just stopped.

Not losing sight of the Bangladeshi worker who had also alighted, Kani told his parents to wait for a few minutes. When Anu pulled him, he said, "Ma, please wait just for a few minutes."

"Can I have a few dollars, Pa?" he said hurriedly keeping an eye on the foreign worker.

Taking out his wallet from his pant pocket, Somu asked impatiently, "But what do you need money so urgently for?" Kani pulled out a ten dollar note.

He pointed to the Bangladeshi standing with a lost expression on his face. "He needs to top up his EZ link, Pa. I heard him cry over the phone. He is broke and in a dire state."

"Don't tell me you can understand their language."

"Oh, I'd say I have been figuring out their language over the year," he said. Always observing, he would smile and wave at the Bangladeshi workers who cleared the garbage chute and cleaned the common areas. But Anu never expected him to have picked up their language.

Kani swiftly went near the foreign worker and asked, "Where do you want to go?"

"Paya Lebar," said the foreign worker, looking at Kani a little hesitantly.

With all kindness, Kani said softly and slowly, "You take the train to Bugis from here. And from there you board the green line towards Pasir Ris, you understand?" The Bangladeshi just nodded shyly.

Gently, Kani thrust the ten dollar note into his hand and hopped back to join his parents. As if trying to prevent them from looking at the Bangladeshis, he pulled them both by his hands. Curiously, He turned to look and was titillated to see the housefly riding on the tattered backpack of the Bangladeshi.

"Eureka! Single pair of wings! Comes under the higher classification of Diptera," he squealed.

***

The Pavilion

It was a Friday afternoon in January. The widespread Neem with several sturdy and innumerable small branches made the atmosphere cool. A couple of dogs growled and fought in the street nearby. From his thatch-roofed sundry shop, Venu watched Naga, Subbu, and Raman who stood in front of the shop talking tirelessly, full of energy.

Venu never talked or looked at the stout Naga ever since he had called him "Cat eyed stupid lame!" a couple of years back when they'd had a bitter tiff. He had struck him on his head with his crutch. Watching them, he wondered how cheerful those boys were, all seventeen, about two years younger than he was.

Seated at one end of the bench, old man Chari, his forehead marked with a red vertical holy line from the bridge of his nose, and the thread across his torso, with 'The Hindu' spread out on his lap said, "Kamaraj Nadar, controlling the Tamil Nadu Congress Committee is a natural kingmaker of Madras Presidency, they say. On the other hand, at the center, it's just five months after independence, and we can already feel we were better off when ruled by the British. My grandfather used to work directly under Sir Thomas Munro as an interpreter. He used to,.."

"You are a shame to our nation." His middle-aged friend Sagayam at the other end of the bench interrupted. With the silver cross hanging from a thin silver chain at his chest, he wore a baggy white shirt and a dhoti.

A host of sparrows flittered skyward from the upper boughs as Chari laughed boisterously in response. "Ha ha ha, I'm only saying that we need stronger leadership." His clean-shaven face glittered with tiny drops of perspiration as he flipped the pages of the previous day's newspaper after adjusting his upper cloth and the tuft at his nape. He handed Sagayam a few sheets that he'd finished reading.

As usual, customers frequented the shop in front of the small red-tile roofed house for their needs of beetle leaves, areca nuts, Wrigley or Orbit peppermint, Lux or Mohan sandal soap, Britania biscuits, and filter cigarettes. Venu would get busier every Wednesday when he had to order goods and help the unlettered rural folks write letters.

When Venu espied freckle-faced Arthur, in pale khaki and white, approaching, he hurriedly caught hold of his underarm crutch placed at the corner. A few partly dried whole sugar canes, the leftover of Pongal, the harvest festival, collapsed on the floor. For a second, contemplating on bending to pick it up, he decided to do it later. 'Tuk,.. tuk' he went up the steps hurriedly into the house, calling his grandfather. The bend at his right ankle made the leg shorter than it should've been, but the contracture at his hip gave him a distorted limp. A family that had come to consult with his grandfather about horoscope matching was leaving.

He waited for a few seconds and said, "*Thaththaa*[20], make sure he leaves immediately," and returned quickly to his seat. "Who?" Venu didn't reply. His cat eyes remind me of mine, Venu thought bitterly.

20 *Thaththaa* - Grandfather

As if continuing from where they had left, Sagayam asked suddenly with approbation "What's wrong with Pundit Nehru's leadership? Gandhiji is there to mentor him."

With derision, Chari said, "Gandhi? Nehru might do better without him. I still remember my visit to Madurai two years back. What a crowd in Race Course ground in Pudur! And in the end, he walks away without giving his speech. The notorious arrogance of the Congress," Chari gave an expression with distorted lips.

"My father was there. That was the fifth time Gandhiji had come to the city, and yet the crowd behaved boisterously. The continuous noise made it impossible for him to make his speech. He appealed to the crowd to stay calm."

"But no one could hear what he said."

The boys were booing at and teasing each other. "You all talk, no action, know only to talk," said Naga, with a serious face. "Beat me in a race before you can open your mouth," said the talkative Subbu. "*Saridaa*, let's swim diagonally from the opposite corner all the way to reach this corner near the shop," Raman planned.

They came to buy three bananas while Naga stood a few yards away staring into space. The trio circumvent the large pond to reach the other corner.

Arthur stood there trying to take a good look at Venu, who eluded his gaze turning his face to stare at the temple pond.

With gentle ripples on the surface, complimenting the mild breeze, the greenish-brown water glittered in the soon to set sunshine. The pond stretched approximately a little more than two hundred meters long and less than two hundred meters wide.

"The microphone on the stage was but a gimmick. The British government purposely didn't supply electricity. So, Gandhiji thought he could still speak if they were silent. But the crowd got anxious when they could not hear him."

"He should've waited. The noise level did come down."

"But, in seconds the crowd was back in full volume. The organizers could not achieve a minimum of silence. So, Gandhi announced that he would not speak."

"You should've seen him stretching his limbs on stage, stubbornly not opening his mouth. Sathyagrahi!" Chari mocked.

"That's a false statement. Gandhiji waited for the crowd to disperse and only then he got up and left the venue quietly."

"Very well informed, aren't you?" Chari said with sarcasm. Looking at the sports section, he commented, "India all out for 58 in Gabba. Late news though, Donald Bradman scored 185 in the Cricket Test."

"Oh!"

"What an expression!" Chari sulked puckishly.

Inside the house, Arthur asked, "Can't he even look at my face?" Grandfather did not reply. Soon Arthur said, "Okay, we should at least get him a forearm crutch. I'm waiting for news from Madras on that. It will be very convenient for him."

"But he wants to save money and buy it himself. And he insists that he's fine with this one," Grandfather replied in a low voice.

"It pains me to see him like this," Arthur said in English, more to himself.

"They diagnosed it as polio only after several weeks, and by then the damage was done. Rest and good food were recommended. But with hardly any food to eat… and nutritious food was a rare commodity in our village up the hill."

"I'm aware of all that. Blame it all on my bad luck that I could not reach out to you sooner."

"My daughter had to die without even taking a look at her newborn.. it saddens me.." Grandfather said wistfully and soon managed to ask, "So when do you plan to leave for Leicester?"

"Clara keeps saying that's not her home and only Kodaikanal is. She says she is more a Tamil than a Briton. Born here, it's natural that she feels this, but it's unbelievable how a thirteen-year-old can talk so clearly and obstinately. I am caught between the mother who longs for her homeland and an adamant daughter. They keep arguing all day."

Grandfather kept silent. But when Arthur said, "I wish to buy this house for Venu," he said hesitantly, "We have no trouble with paying the rent."

On the bench, Sagayam continued where they had left, "And when Gandhiji addressed a public meeting in Upper Coonoor, people had walked miles from estates and villages to see him. He'd stayed at Mount Pleasant." Chari just nodded.

"Gandhi signed in the visitor's book at the Meenakshi Amman temple on that visit. He wrote, 'I am happy; my longtime desire has been fulfilled.' Harijans were allowed into the temple. Thakkar Baba accompanied him. V.I.Munuswamy Pillai also went along with them. He belongs to my village."

Without looking up, but with a mild cynicism Chari said, "And Nadar quietly followed along wherever Gandhi went those days."

The boys plunged into the pond together with a jubilant cheer followed by a big thud from the shop. Everyone involuntarily turned to glance.

"One gram of gold costs eight rupees eighty six paise, and yet we get to see ladies adorning head to feet with gold," Chari said. They were looking at a pair of newlyweds who walked a few feet apart from each other on the other side of the road. The chocolate complexioned young girl, clad in a bright red sari, with a long oiled plait touching her knee, face bent to look down at her feet as if searching for a needle on the road, walked behind her husband.

"I've never in my life heard of gold sold at such high price."

"People are heading to watch *Nam Iruvar*, first show. Have you watched?" showing his two fingers Chari nodded in affirmation. "Twice." He had just started his ceremonious betel leaves munching.

Venu heard Arthur telling grandfather, "Clara's mother insists she would go back alone if required. She suspects I am inclined to stay back for Venu's sake."

"I think you should convince the child and go back. I'm here to take good care of him. Not to worry."

"Clara is unaware of having a half-brother. Her mother in the depth of her heart has a soft corner for Venu but opposes my idea of introducing Clara to him. And we would have to start from scratch if we go back. Selling off all the properties here would still not suffice."

The pavilion in the middle had a shot tower that looked almost dilapidated. Subbu and Raman went up holding on to the solid structure, upon reaching the shelter to lie down to rest on the floor with legs and hands spread out, as if crucified. They marveled at the panoptic view from there.

Gesturing towards the pyol of the house Venu smiled at Ismail who came in his bullock cart to unload the sacks of goods. He turned to watch the pond.

Naga swam forward slowly as he looked back at his buddies. Burned out, he seemed to struggle. Must be muscular cramps, Venu feared. "Any of you swim?" he asked generally facing the customers and the duo seated on the bench.

Shaking their heads, "No," both of them said in unison. "But you only know to talk big and fat," Venu thought. "Wait a while. I'll come and pay you," he said to Ismail as he suddenly got up.

"*Thaththaa*, look after the shop," he shouted as he grabbed his crutch and hurried.

"It's not as if this is the only shop around. I can get my cigarette anywhere," a troubled youth said aloud as he mounted on his bicycle and pedaled away.

Tuk,... tuk,... tuk...bare feet Venu looked dauntless as he went fast down the steps. Leaving the crutch in a hurry, he dived right into the water to swim fast towards the middle.

Ready to plunge, Arthur asked stupefied with a worry, "Can he really swim?" Pulling him back Venu's grandfather said calmly "Yes, he can."

Naga sank deep twice to surge back up to the surface with a splash. With hands turning rag-like, his head was slightly visible every few seconds. Having gulped a lot of water he seemed almost to drown. An astonished crowd gathered to watch.

Subbu and Raman were standing at the central pavilion shouting, "Naga, Naga!" Trying to caution them, Sagayam shouted at the top of his voice, "Stay right there. Don't jump into the water!"

Ismail untied the bulls from the cart and tied them to the tree leaving a bunch of fresh green grass for them before rushing to join the crowd.

Halfway, Venu swam fast. With a short pause in his forward stroke, he decelerated, as if to tap out most of the efficiency, glided forward. He accelerated immediately but with much difficulty. His adapted swimming astonished all those watched. He reached the place where Naga was struggling to surface.

The crowd started speculating on who would survive. "Neither," said many.

"*Poomaa, poo. Malli, mullappoo,*" a flower seller walked briskly balancing the shallow basket of jasmine strings on her head. Unable to contain her curiosity, she joined the crowd to take a look.

Many pedestrians, cart drivers, cyclists, and a motorist, stopped to join the crowd.

Near the pavilion, Venu pulled Naga to the surface and slapped him twice holding his head by his hair, but Naga did not open the eyes. Panting for breath, Venu pulled him by his tuft and swam back swiftly. The crowd watched spellbound when the boys disappeared under water more than once.

As soon as Venu reached the steps, a group lifted Naga. Pressing his stomach hard could not help, and so Ismail's bullock cart was turned sideways, and Naga was tied flat facing down on the wheel with a rope and rotated very fast.

Soon, Naga vomited water with all the undigested banana and biscuits. When he opened his eyes, he looked frightened. Soon Naga's mother and sister came wailing. The temple bell started ringing for the next few seconds when most of them scurried towards the temple.

Exhausted, attempting to gather himself, with eyes closed Venu laid on the bottom-most step. With pond water all around, it looked like he was floating in still water. Arthur rushed near him and watched his tall, slender structure with a tanned complexion, his wet clothes rising up and down in rhythm.

Hesitating, he picked up the crutch and left it reachable near his right hand. With no one around, he bent down to say, "It's okay if you won't call me 'father,' but I did not betray your mother. I swear by God! You'll understand one day that it was the rough play of destiny."

Venu's grandfather ascended the steps with a large glass of steaming rich coffee in hand when Arthur climbed up the steps looking around.

With the sun almost down, slowly darkness crept in. The stench of dung and cattle urine filled the air as Ismail tied his bulls back to the cart.

The youth with the bicycle returned to the shop, "My folks at home are weeping," he said and continued to announce, "Did you hear the latest news on the radio? Gandhiji has been shot at Birla house in Delhi, just an hour back." After looking sharply at Ismail for a few seconds, he went on to add, "They say it's a Muslim who has shot him," and rushed off as if he had been assigned the duty to convey the news to the whole town.

Ismail looked worried, and his frightened face looked skyward showing up both his palms "Ya Allah!"

"That's most unlikely. In all the previous attempts, very distinctly, only Hindus were involved. I am sure, a Muslim would not have shot at Gandhi," Arthur said reassuringly as he watched Venu sauntering to his shop. Tuk,… tuk,… tuk… He was more intrigued than ever before by the bright glow in his eyes in the dark, that resembled his own.

***

Dangling Gandhi

When Ram helped his father to the rear seat of the cab, Kumar held the old man on the other side. "*Appa*, you board in front," Kumar said as he sat left to his grandfather. "Mount Elizebeth hospital, please."

Ram texted his son a frisky message in WhatsApp: *How I love such rare chances of long rides when I don't need to be at the wheels, thanks to the delay at the service station.*

After smiling at Kumar through the rare view mirror, Ram looked keenly at the beige coloured bust figurine that dangled above the dashboard and then gave an intrigued smile. The driver said, "He is lucky for me." The name card stuck on the interior of the window shield said he was Derick Tan. He drove northeast.

"But do you know who this is?"

"Ya *lah*. Gandhi. An old friend who visited India a few years back brought back this souvenir."

"He not only preached nonviolence but lived his ideology to show the world. My dad, though a critic of Gandhi, is his namesake."

'Vaishnava Jana tho thene kahiye jhe, PeeD paraayi jaaNe re'

Derrick looked a little inquisitively at the reclined wrinkly figure through the rearview. "That's the favourite song of Gandhi," Ram tried to explain. "It means - he and he alone is the man of God, who knows the pain and the misery of others."

"Shall I switch on the 96.8fm?"

"Sorry but we're not interested in Tamil FM."

"Kiss 92fm?"

"Yes," said Kumar and, "No," said Ram simultaneously in a hurry. The driver laughed courteously. "Switch off?"

"Thanks."

"Is your father unwell? Do you want the air con reduced?" he asked prudently.

"Used to air con that he is, he should be fine. He is mostly reminiscing. We are on our way to walk him through his annual health check," Interestingly, Ram started liking Derrick.

The temple, hundreds of years old, with a couple of large Marutham trees, with buttressed trunks, a male and a female said to cure heart diseases, stood one each on north and south banks of the Varaha river.

After the Perumal temple, North agraharam and the South agraharam, both reasonably wide, ran parallel to each other and towards. As we walk a few kilometers past the bus stand in the main road we can reach the temple, and down the steps, one can touch the gently flowing waters of the big river.

Since early morning jubilant celebrations of independence were in full swing all over the town. Most of the households had simple payasam, a sweet pudding made out of the British rationed rice and some simple floral decorations within their means.

The auspicious music of the nadaswaram , along with the heavy rhythms of the drums from the gramophones blasting in the loud speakers in the open ground added to the austerity. One-sided papers crudely stuck together and circumspectly painted with watercolour and colour pencils to form tri coloured flags adorned the front of the houses. Joyful excitement and undefined expectation filled the air.

Turning left at Bukit Panjang Road, the taxi went straight first and swirled to slide around into the BKE that stretched about two kilometers.

As if half asleep, the grandfather murmured, "Lakshmi, can you give me my small pillow?" Kumar asked very softly, "*Thaathaa*[21], are you okay?" Slightly opening his eyes, the old man gave a very slight affirmative nod and a crooked smile. Ram turned to look back. "He is reminded of my mother. But wonder why all of a sudden after so many years?" he said with a tone of concern to his son in Tamil.

"Do you understand Tamil?"
"No *lah*," Derrick laughed loudly. "I wish I could."

"My son speaks Mandarin fairly well."

Kumar gave a deliberate cough to indicate his displeasure, for which his father scorned mildly with a contrite grin.

"Oh, that's very quiet good. Young people, these days are smart. I have heard my father talk Tamil. My grandfather came from China in his teens, worked as coolie for an affluent merchant who had a big shop near the Singapore River. Father had a childhood friend called Kuppu, who joined the INA[22].

"Bose called it *Azad Hind Fauj*."

21 *Thaathaa* - grandfather
22 INA - Indian National Army

"It seems father missed him so much but never heard of him after that."

"Oh how sad!"

"My dad used to work as a janitor in Cathay Cinema hall. I heard that's where Netaji proclaimed the provision of 'free India' and after two days declared war on the US and Britain and with the help of the then ruling Japanese. He went on a recruitment drive. Those days Cathay Cinema hall, one of the tallest of buildings in Singapore, was the center for the British colonial as well as the Japanese rule."

Pointing at the dangling Gandhi with the toothless and hence innocent smile he asked Derrick, "What else do you know of him?"

"Oh, not much, Sir,.."

"My son here would not know even what you might know," he interrupted to tease. Kumar gave a pugnacious glare at his father.

".. except that he brings me good luck," Derrick completed.

"Like the laughing Buddha, you mean?"

"A sentiment of that kind, you can say. Gandhi said, 'Nature and the greens are not our inheritance from our ancestors, but they are on loan from our future generations, right?"

"Oh! So, you watch Channel New Asia."

"Ha, ha, ha! Once in a while, lah. When I rest at home, I like to watch 'The family affair,' 'A house of its time' and such series."

"It's amazing that almost a century back Gandhi was so clear about the importance of using our natural resources wisely."

Kumar's WhatsApp said: '*Appa, as always you have forgotten your promise that you won't indulge in any conversation with the taxi driver.*'

Ram made an amused eye contact with him on the rare view.

The taxi sped under the Eco Bridge, the first connecting biodiversity in South East Asia, connecting the Bukit Timah Nature Reserve to the catchment Nature Reserve.

"Isn't it beautiful!"

"Yeah, at 16 million dollars!"

"But every single sapling nurtured is for the future."

"Varaha, the third incarnation of the boar faced Lord Vishnu could not possibly happen in this era to save his consort, mother Earth," The old man murmured in Tamil.

"What's he saying?" Derrick asked a little serious faced.

"Oh, the importance of saving our Earth."

***

A cool breeze brushed the body. Along the banks of the Varaha with the slowly setting sun, the silhouettes of those clad in dhoti, men of all ages with forehead tonsure and tufts of various sizes at the nape of their necks, engaged in their daily ritual of evening sun salutation, made a picturesque sight. With the holy threads across their torsos, they offered the river water with both hands, with chants, facing the sun.

Amongst the young children playing around merrily, only a few infantile girls were seen. Some children played with sand. They let the fine, slightly moist, soft and sand from their palms through the fingers as they talked, watched. There were no female adults.

"Madras Presidency of British India, they say, would be split into different states. Will Periyakulam taluk remain in Madurai District after that?"

"I will badly miss my boss, James Prescott. What a gem of a person he is! He says his young children are not willing to migrate to Birmingham. They are begging to stay."

Men of all ages sat in groups mostly talking about politics. "Right from 'June 3 plan' the astrologers across the country were outraged because 15th August for them was an unfortunate and unholy date."

"But Lord Mountbatten has been adamant on that date. They say it's his lucky date."

"That's why the astrologers suggested the midnight hour between Aug 14 and 15 because as per the Hindu calendar, a new day starts only at sunrise, you see."

"Nehru delivered his speech exactly between 11:51 pm and 12:39 am last night."

"To mark the independence of thc nation, the holy conch was blown at the strike of twelve. Did you tune your radio?" boasted a young man from an affluent family. His six-year-old daughter went round and round to watch her bright blue ankle silk skirt with golden brocades swell balloon-like. "Sit here, Lakshmi. The sand falls on everyone, can't you see?"

"Oh, the valves of mine have given away weeks back. I need to get them fixed," said his friend.

"Why don't you accept that you don't have the power supply?" he laughed.

"Then, why did you come here for the news?" teased the other. "Mohan, instead of sitting here watching the elders talk, why don't you go and play with her?" he asked his son.

"Of course, to talk with you all." There were cheerful chattering and laughter all around.

"Getting independence the day before the new moon day bothers Sasthri, our neighbour. He strongly believes it would have been much better if the big day was tomorrow instead."

"But look at Ibrahim Ravuthar, the tailor there! He is happily wearing the tricolor flag on his shirt rushing to the mosque for his Friday evening prayer." Salim, his puerile son, waved happily to his classmate Mohan.

'Aaduvome pallu paaduvome'[23] The group discussions subsequently stopped when the Municipality loudspeaker started blasting national songs one after the other for the next half an hour. The ebullient atmosphere set many of them to join in singing.

Before the sunset, the news broadcast. "Sir Archibald Edward Nye stepped down as the Governor of Madras yesterday, and O.P. Ramaswamy Reddiyar takes office as the first Chief Minister of the state."

***

When the taxi exited at Whitley Road, Ram asked, "Do you know that Gandhi stayed years in South Africa?"

"No," Derrick said shyly.

"The seed of freedom fight was sowed in him when he was there."

Appa, will you stop boasting your knowledge of your high school history? Regret coming with you. Now, stop being so coltish.

Putting away his mobile into his shirt pocket, Ram asked, "How long have you been driving a cab?"

"For about five or six years."

---

23 *'Aaduvome pallu paaduvome'* – Lets dance and sing to celebrate, one of the many Indian national song in Tamil, written to celebrate Indian independence by the great poet Bharathi long before the big day.

"And before that?"

"I did nothing much actually, despite my business degree. I have been in and out of jobs. All thanks to the wrong company at my younger age, addictively, I gambled away for many years until I lost everything inherited and earned," he said without any sign of remorse.

"Which part of the island do you reside in?"

"I live in Whampoa."

"Children must have grown up."

"All three are grown up. My youngest girl should be about your son's age," he pointed to the back seat.

How could you assume so shamelessly, pa? What if he had no kids? I won't board a taxi with you ever again my life, I swear.'

Politely Ram nodded to his right and then turned to his left to watch the roadside through the window.

"Are you from India, Sir?"

"Oh, we came here before this guy was born, that's about 22 years back," he waved his hand backward.

"Then you are a local already."

"Yeah, you could say that."

"But you don't look or talk like one. I thought you had migrated recently to Singapore."

Pride written all over his face, Ram smiled at Derick with gratification.

Happy? Accomplished your triumphant target of having preserved your identity and the roots?

They turned into Stevens Road after Whitley Road when Ram asked, "Is your wife also employed?"

"My ex-wife, I hope she is employed."

"Oh…"

"We are divorced."

This century's biggest divorce is happening in Europe, and here you are talking about the story of one of the millions of common divorces. And an Empire that so firmly believed in dividing and ruling is on the verge of a division.

"Sorry."

"That's okay. It's been more than a decade now, since the year I went to prison for causing severe hurt to a guy in a loan shark-related fight. All that I earn so hard to go for the alimony and the endless debts. I get to eat my simple meals."

A tense silence fell for the next few minutes. Gliding out of Scotts Road, the taxi turned left into Orchard Road. *'I have a question for both you men; do you know the name of our senior Lee's mother?'* Reading WhatsApp, Ram turned to look searchingly at Kumar, who with pressed lips widened his eyes. As he paid in cash for the taxi fare, he asked Derrick, "Do you know our LKY's mother's name?"

The driver looked blank for seconds before twisting to stretch out his right hand to give the change, "Thanks, Sir. It was great talking to you." He smiled.

Controlling his laughter, Kumar said looking first at the driver and then at his father, "Chua Jim Neo."

"Oh, okay."

After getting out Kumar called out, "*Thaththaa*, we have reached." There was no response of any kind. Attempting to shake him gently,

Kumar touched his arm. It felt icy cold and lifeless. With a clouded face, he looked up at his father skittishly.

Ram asked, "What?"

***

Read Singapore!

With the midcourse exams around the corner, I wanted to believe that I was sincerely finding ways and means to get into the studying mode. Sustained concentration had become difficult for me of late. My mind that found immense satisfaction in composing small pieces on guitar, drifted away too fast into the world of music. Furthermore, I had gotten bored with the usual study table in my room and the surroundings, and I was inclined to believe that was one of the causes of the problem. So, I hoped the atmosphere in the public library could do some magic. My mind contemplated on the idea of going over to the main branch in Victoria Street, where the chances of finding a suitable place to settle were more. To save travel time, I decided to go to Ang Mo Kio library.

Just when I collected my files and notebook to leave, my mother who hardly sends me on any errand asked me to borrow one particular Tamil book for herself. She, a voracious reader, visits the library religiously at least once a week. Though she would try reading my suggestions of Eoin Colfer's Artemis Fowl series or Dan Brown, her taste matched better with Maria Nehmat's 'Prisoner Of Tehran,' Khaled Hossein's 'Thousand Splendid Suns,' Jung Chang's 'Wild Swans,' Anitha Nair's Ladies Coupe and such.

As always when I said in English, "I'm afraid I may not have time to comb through shelves to locate that title, A*mma*," she replied in Tamil, "Oh, come on Raghu, that's one of the two Tamil titles chosen for this year's 'Read Singapore.' So, it should be straightforward to find it *da*." She repeated the title and author's name. Though recognizing and reading my mother tongue was never a problem, I doubted if I could still read Tamil as well as before. But I did not say anything. Reading just a title and an author's name should not be difficult, I thought.

When I got off the bus, I realized that it was neither too hot nor cloudy. The aroma of fries and burger from the drive-in McDonald's flew with the gentle breeze. Traffic was scarce and smooth in that main road. Fairly grown healthy trees along the road divider and the very aged trees with their large crowns on the two sides of the avenue provided ample shade. The Ang Mo Kio Town Garden on the mound had a flight of stairs leading up to the well maintained lush garden. There were palm trees with uniform heights grown on the two sides of the steps. There was a lotus pond filled with big green, fresh and healthy leaves. Lovely pink lotuses complementing the green were partially visible from the road. I brushed aside my urge to go up to savor the beauty from near. As I walked to take the overhead bridge, I could see a few people heading towards the library. From there the pond was vivid.

There stood near the book drop a Chinese girl, holding her books waiting for her turn. Her face looked familiar. The moment she glanced at me and smiled hesitantly I remembered her name Xinyi, from my secondary school. I returned her smile. Even after two full years, she didn't seem to have changed much in appearance. For a second, I didn't know if I should halt to speak a few words to her even though we weren't close friends in school. But, when she didn't bother about all that and continued to drop her books, I decided to go on my way.

At the entrance on the left was the information counter where there were two members of the staff serving the readers who had queued up. It was interesting to note that some readers picked one of the grey coloured baskets similar to those used by the shoppers in supermarkets. There were many children engrossed in their reading, choosing books and talking in various tones. "I choose this one," said a young Chinese boy of about six. Trying to snatch away the book, "No. I choose first", said the other older boy who looked like his brother. There came their mother saying in an authoritative but low voice, "*Sh,. Its ok boy boy. Cannot shout one. Quiet in the library, okay? Just borrow lah. Both also can read, wha?*" After choosing, the trio went away to the borrowing kiosk.

I went up the stairs. The sofas on the left were all occupied. A few senior citizens were up-dating their knowledge of current affairs, reading the dailies. There were some who immersed in their books, as well as a few who were sleeping with their eyes open. Perhaps, the reading brings in them sleep. Some restless teens were pretending to study. They were seated along the walls on the floor. The tables were filled with papers, laptops, and files of the students. The environment sure gives an inspiration, I thought. But, I wondered if I would be able to find a place to sit. I thought I would try the first floor and the area near the cafeteria. Before that, I should first borrow the book for mom lest I forget about it later.

When I entered the famous Indian section that consisted mainly of Tamil books, I was amused to see a few toddlers were meddling with the ornamental miniatures of the Indian musical instruments like the *tabla, Veena,* and *nadaswaram*. 'Please refrain from using or playing these instruments as they are meant for decoration only' - read the notice there which seemed to be a recent addition. I remembered seeing a few teens playing with them, 'dhom, dhom' and 'dhuk dhuk,' once long before during one of my earlier visits. Multimedia and the magazine sections of this place had fewer readers browsing. I seemed to feel handicapped as I didn't know how to look for the book. I texted, 'Mom, I'm afraid I might not be able to find the book. I doubt if I can read Tamil. It's almost two years since I stopped studying Tamil'. She replied, 'You can. How can a Language learnt for more than ten years be forgotten?'

In a few more seconds she had messaged, 'Do you think anyone will believe that you have completed your AO level Tamil with a distinction?' I couldn't help laughing. When I asked her with a smile, where to look for the title, she replied immediately to look under 'SAA' and 'KAN.' There was no one near the bookshelves when I searched those two call numbers.

When I spotted one of *Sujatha*'s books under 'SUJ,' I was reminded of my secondary school days, especially the Tamil lessons. While drafting essays in Tamil, most of us in school used to feel lost mainly because we always thought in English and translated every sentence into Tamil. So, we used to get stuck when we could not come up with an equivalent Tamil word. Mrs.Rajan, who taught us Higher Tamil used to insist on reading Tamil books and short stories to improve our vocabulary. That was when I tried reading some Tamil books when science fiction by *Sujatha* appealed to me the most. The teacher always used to insist, "First of all, you must believe that Tamil is not as hard or bitter as you think." When the spoken form of the language was encouraged by the MOE for our Oral exams, our translating minds became all the more uncomfortable. The Tamil feature film recommended, never helped us as they had themes, slang, and dialects of South India, which was not a bit relevant to Singapore, very unfamiliar to the local students. Tamil classes were fun and exciting otherwise.

A library employee, who was sorting books on the shelves, passed by. I approached her asking, "Could you please help me? I want to,..", Only to be interrupted by her. "You look on the shelves. Or you can ask at the reception counter at the entrance", she said and walked away. Another Indian staff came by smilingly asking me if I needed help. When I told her the title and author's name, she went to the shelves to check. "Did you check if there are copies in this branch?" She asked, to which I said, "No. I'll check right away. Thanks."

As I reached the catalogue, I thought I should've written down the title and author name immediately after mom told them. Of course, I did remember it was *Sooriyavamsam* by *Sa.Kandasami*, but I was not too confident in spelling them both. I chose the Tamil font in the system. As I typed the title, I wondered if it should be 'su' or 'soo.'

In two years, I had nearly forgotten the language which I had studied almost reluctantly. What a waste! Or was it? Wouldn't it be cool to brag around elsewhere when I migrate in the future, that I knew one of the classical languages?

'Su' or 'soo'? Let me think. Well, since it is *Sooriyavamsam,* it should be 'soo,' I decided. I could always try the search again with 'su.' Therefore, I added that cursive stroke for the 'su.' The system was kind enough to show the title immediately. So, I didn't have to bother with spelling the author's name correctly.

I wondered why there was not a single copy on the shelf when there are seventeen copies available in the branch. I decided to go down to the reception to ask. Before leaving I headed towards the washroom near the photocopying area. A few people were reading in the soundproof room. I could see through the glass walls that there were a few sofas empty. But, the most profound silence and the low temperature inside wouldn't suit me. So, I looked around to see if there was an empty place. There was one table with four chairs. I decided to rush to grab a chair. However, after relieving myself, when I returned, I found the table occupied by four friends.

Now that there was no place for me to sit and study, I thought I might as well go down to check with the staff at the reception. I descended the flight of stairs. Many readers were walking here and there. Except for a couple who was paying their fines, most of them were browsing and searching their reads either on the shelves or on-screen catalogues. Some children were merely playing games on computers.

There were one Chinese lady and a Malay lady at the counter. I ended up with the Malay lady who smiled at me and asked, "Yes, what can I do for you?" I said I was looking for one particular Tamil book and that the chosen book for the 'Read Singapore' is available but not to be seen on the shelf. She tried to find another Indian staff who could help me, but she was on medical leave. Saying, "I am sorry. But, there are no Tamil librarians at the moment. However, I will try to help you", she was hesitating how to go about it.

I waited. Library staff was pushing the trolley containing books and magazines to sort and place them according to their call numbers. A couple followed by their two kids approached her to ask where their books could be located. She guided them and turned towards a lady who looked like an expatriate who asked very politely if there was a washroom on the first floor. Most of the area was occupied by the shelves containing countless books for the children of all ages varying from the washable plastic picture books for less than one-year-olds to Enid Blyton, comics, Famous Fives, and Secret Sevens. Children pulled the books at their whim and fancy. Some were chosen and placed in the basket. But many were left them scattered on the floor, on the chairs, tables, sofas as well as on wrong shelves. The staff who patiently went around collecting and arranging them on the respective shelves amazed me. I wished I had half that patience with my books and files.

Despite the regular announcement by the staff over the speaker every few hours to remind the readers to keep silence in the library, the children in their excitement raised their voices while talking. The volume went higher and higher as time passed. Some adults weren't exceptions. Upon hearing the announcement, they begin to whisper, only to start talking loudly after some time.

The librarian came back to tell me, "Sir, I think my colleague can help you." The Chinese lady who was naturally courteous asked me, "Could you please write in this paper the title and author's name so that I can go up to the storeroom to check if the book can be located? Please write in big letters", she said. I wrote the title and the author's name boldly and checked if I wrote the correct spelling. "The title is spelt correctly, though I am not too sure of the spelling of the author's name," I said. "Never mind. Please give me some time. I will do my best", she said hurriedly and left for the lift. Many readers were waiting behind me. So,

I left the queue and walked to the cafeteria where there were a few empty chairs. Seated there, I looked around. The road under the bright sun was visible through the transparent glass wall.

A Malay girl about the age of seven was sipping her orange juice while her father paid. Turning around he said, "*Can not see only picture picture. Must read also, ok? Must read everyday one. You finish one book I give you one star. Like that like that, you have ten stars, I bring you to McDonald's. Never read, then cannot. Ok?*" Busy with her drink she didn't say anything. She tagged behind her father as he walked. He bent down to look at her face to ensure that she was listening as he repeated the same again. She nodded her head more to stop him from repeating the same.

The tall shelves with fiction for adults stood near the right wall behind the cafeteria. The tables were all occupied but for one. The apron-clad employees were serving a little food and beverage items such as noodles, potato wedges, hot chocolates, and coffee. Some were drinking while studying while others were eating after having finished with their studying or note taking. A few students in school uniforms seemed busy with their homework.

I pulled out my file and opened the chapter on vectors. With no Indian staff around to help, I wondered how she was going to locate the book. Perhaps, she was only trying to be polite, I thought. Every few seconds I set sight on the reception counter to know if she had returned. I made sure I would be visible to her when she comes looking for me.

As soon as I saw her coming, I got up to reach her. "Is this the title, sir?", She asked me courteously. She was holding the book with white lettering on the black colored wrapper. I looked at the book cover which had the letters somewhat distorted in trying to be artistic and was pleasantly surprised that it was indeed the title. "Yes, thank you," I said.

"The chosen titles are yet to be shelved. Sorry for the inconvenience."

I smiled and asked, "Oh, that's Ok. Thank you very much. How did you manage to recognize the book? You read Tamil?"

She felt shy and simply said, "No *lah*. I just matched the characters", and walked away, back to her place. After the first few seconds of overwhelming moments, inspired by her dedication and sincerity and at the same time felt slightly ashamed. I could almost hear Mrs.Rajan, and our Tamil teacher says, "If we are not going to learn our language, then who will? *sollunga*, m?"

After revising a substantial amount of physics on that day, I left the library premises late in the evening. While returning home by bus, I pulled out the Tamil book from my bag. I read the first two pages of the novel and felt that I could decipher neither the theme nor the plot.

When mother took the book from me as she opened the door, I asked her, "Have you any idea what this novel is about?" She shook her head sideways to say 'no.' When I said, "From the first two pages it's difficult to figure out anything at all," she stared at me with her mouth open. "You mean you read on your way?"

I nodded.

***

Mother

Umthleh, Shillong
30th August 1866

My dearest Maria, I hope this letter reaches you on time. Although I haven't received yours for the month, I decided to write again.

As I lie on the mat with my half-filled pipe smoking, watching the soft gurgling waters of Umjasai, at an altitude of 1496 meters, I miss you intensely. Believe me; we have a Scotland right here but far less cold and therefore salubrious. Given its beauty and the climatic conditions, it is very slowly becoming not just a refuge for our officers and staff but a popular destination for their families. With school and hospital being constructed, it has expanded to about more than four square miles and becoming more of a small town.

The natives continue to refer to it as Yeodo. Please continue to put that within the brackets for a few more months, just in case. The military offices and post offices are almost used to the new name. It's been months since the Government of Bengal has acculturated to 'Shillong.'

It has taken our side decades of insidious efforts to control the Khasi uprising, I learn. All thanks to Colonel Henry Hopkinson who found this village of two square miles with a population of barely a thousand around the weekly market, and after almost 30 years of being just a sanatorium, we have managed to possess this heaven on Earth after the Khasi leader's surrender to our military. As it is in the process of becoming the capital of Assam, it continues to display subtle residues of the two Burmese wars. Many soldiers who came to convalesce here have not left the place.

Our Joanna is going to adore Shillong positively. She can start her schooling here. Did she like the globe mama bought for her? Mama described in her last letter that she had planned to buy a bigger one and that Joanna insisted on getting only the cricket ball sized.

Maria, you will refuse to leave India after you come here. Unlike our place, we can own the land we want to and perhaps build a large bungalow to your liking. Please don't disappoint me this time and let me book your tickets. Just tell me if I should come to Bombay or to Calcutta to receive you.

As always yours lovingly,
Leonard Ashworth

***

"Why can't I go to their house?" Gloria had asked that countless time just as tirelessly as Nanny used to start the story of the doe from the plains to divert her attention.

"Do you remember what happened to U Sier Lapalang from Bangla when he wanted to go to unknown lands, Khun?"

Cutting her *Kwai*, the areca nut with the small cutter from her waist pouch she would continue, "He came here to Khasi hills looking for adventure. His mother came searching for him. She sang yearningly where ever she went looking for him. He wandered around for food not knowing that a group of hunters was waiting for him." She would start munching the cut nuts will betel leaves.

The nanny who belonged to the Hynniewtrep community always wore *Dhara*. She would refer to U Sier Lapalang as if it were a human rather than a deer. The skeleton of the story about the four main rivers originating from Shillong peak and their nine streams would always be the same, varying only in some of the nuances of the muscle and skin she developed every time to suit her moods and that of her audience, none other than Gloria.

Most of the times to avoid the place where the deer died Gloria would jump to, "The mother doe crossed thousands of miles in search of her son. Wailing all the way finally she reached Shyllong peak. The God of Shyllong 'U Lei Shyllong' waged his staff on her head, and spring came pouring out in her place. Only a person who genuinely thirsts for it can find the magical spring."

Nanny would laugh displaying all her brown crooked teeth. "Really! Others cannot see it; you must believe it."

When Gloria said, "I want to climb up the Shillong peak and see if I can view the spring." Nanny would nod a yes.

Other times, Gloria would adamantly ask, "Why can't I go to the Malki park on my own? It is just across the road."

If Nanny asked her, "If you get lost who will come searching for you?" Gloria would absentmindedly say, "My Grandpa."

"But how can he?"

"Then, you will come and search for me."

"I am getting old, and I can't." Nanny would laugh.

"Grandpa's leg will grow long and then he will be able to come for me."

"And what if both his legs grow longer?" Nanny would try to joke.

Gloria would ignore her, "I want to go there now," and stamp her foot obstinately making a long face.

"We shall go for a walk in the evening," Nanny would try to mollify her. "Grandpa might join us."

"Now!" She would try harder.

As she grew up, Gloria stopped listening to Nanny's stories as she found them not as fascinating as before.

***

"Aaaaachchu!" Mother Cecil sneezes, and the class laughs. "What's so funny about a person sneezing?" Quiet. After watching the few stealthy side glances of the zip-lipped control of the girls, Mother continues her Moral science lesson.

Suddenly, Mother sneezes again. The class laughs all over again, louder this time. Her eyes spread full as she sternly says, "Class, get up!" The commotion of tables and chairs brush against the floor, a few bangs here and a few screeches here and there amidst giggles. After three full minutes, witnessing Mother's glare, the girls come to a standstill. Mother continues. She starts on the next chapter on the civics of urban life, the ethics of the mass.

"Aaaaachchu!" Mother sneezes louder and stronger than before, and the class laughs louder than the second time. She gets furious but remains silent staring at the faces of the students, a few seconds on each. Minutes pass by as she moves her gaze from one face to another scanning through. When she sneezes the fourth time, the class bursts laughing uncontrollably. That's when Mother gets up and yells, "Get out of my class this minute!" Suddenly falling silent, the girls hesitate a few seconds. "I said leave the classroom!"

The girls file in a shabby single row as they leave the classroom. Various expressions are evident on their faces, but most of them are giggling secretly. Slowly Mother follows them. "Go down and stand in the middle of the ground," she gestures pointing to the vast ground under the gloomy grey sky. It happens to be one of those colder late October days, the chill almost unbearable even during the hours of noon. The exposed skin between the edges of the navy blue woolen pinafore and the long white socks show goosebumps. Keeping the legs together and rubbing the palms don't help. The teachers from other classrooms step out of their doors to take a quick peek beyond the corridors' waist-high parapet walls.

After minutes, when the bell rings, "Stand right where you are," says Mother and returns to the class to take her books and stationery. With rosary hanging from the large right pocket of her black robe, she walks down the stairs wearing the sweater, "The class will not disperse until Sister Thomas comes here," she says sternly to Madhumitha, the class monitor as she walks towards the other block of classrooms on the higher mound.

Mother sneezes twice on her way as she walks across the vast ground. "Does she even remember that she is the Vice Principal?" The class watches her back and starts whispering and chattering once she is out of listening range. Mother involuntarily halts and looks back at the girls before she continues to ascend the flight of stairs. She stands for a few seconds on the second topmost steps to take yet another look at the girls.

After about five minutes, Sister Thomas, the Principal comes with Mother. "Aren't you all old enough to behave like young ladies?" she asks authoritatively. "Aaaaachchu!" Mother sneezes. Her nose turns red as a fresh ripe tomato. The girls suppress their laughter. Intrigued by the expression on their faces, Sister Thomas turns around to glance at Mother and ends up controlling her laughter too.

***

The Times

19th June 1897

London: Shillong, a hill town in the North East part of India faced an earthquake, 8.8 on the Richter scale that devastated the hill town into an enormous pile of rubble and woods last Saturday. The Viceroy to the Secretary of State in London reported details of the damages in Shillong, Guwahati and the region. With 27 lives lost, the mortality rate was not high, but the property damages were too substantial. Water pipes were damaged all over creating fountains of water that led to flooding. The tea gardens in Assam and Cachar, Shillong, Guwahati, Goalpara, and Dhubri were all destroyed. The towns of Dibrugarh, Tezpur, and Mangaldai, were unscathed. Due to the complete breakdown of telegraphs and other means of communication, reports from Assam were delayed. The Courts, the Treasuries, jails, and hospitals were destroyed all over Assam. The loss of food supplies was enormous, and the crops were significantly damaged. An unnamed district town nearby lost 750 lives.

***

Shillong

29th September 1897

Dear Mama,

Hope your mobility has not been affected much by your illness.

I have recovered well, and therefore I decided to write to you myself instead of seeking other's help. Hope you will be happy to know that I am getting used to walking with the crutches.

My experience on the day of the earthquake keeps haunting me, and I continue to get nightmares. It was a rainy day when suddenly our bungalow swayed violently like a ship in a severe storm. The ground was on huge waves.

Maria was in the church for her weekly volunteering. Joanna was in our kitchen. "Joanna run out!" I shouted as I ran out of the house carrying the eleven months old Gloria. Before I reached the portico, I felt the building tumbling over me. Joanna would have survived if only she had run out of the back door, but she could not reach across the living room to the front entrance. It was a miracle that Gloria and I were found alive the next day. I was unconscious embracing Gloria like a bird guarding its nestling within its broad spread wings. And she was holding Joanna's globe in her right hand. She must have grabbed it involuntarily as I ran past the study table.

I remember watching with terror the surface of a glass of water standing on a table.. in a constant state of tremor, as I lay with the amputated left leg on the hospital bed. There were 561 aftershocks until the end of the 15th of June, 125 between 15th to 30th June, and 84 from 1st to 15th July. Most of the aftershocks were not felt over a large area but were confined locally.

Memories of Maria and Joanna crush my spirits day and night. Losing my leg was nothing compared to losing them both. Gloria keeps alive that bit of desire in me to live.

Nothing of our church remained except rubble. People had countless stories to tell. Brick constructions were all razed to the ground. Boiling hot water was springing from newly formed volcanoes, in the most unexpected places at the most unexpected times not just along the roadsides, the fields, and grounds but also amidst the rubble. Some of them were throwing up the dark, red sand, and grey ashes. The earthquake left an area of 150,000 square miles in ruins and was felt over one and a quarter million square miles from the Western Burmese border to almost near Delhi. Railway tracks, tramways were severely damaged in many parts of the region.

Sorry mama, thanks for your concern but I am not leaving Shillong because I can't feel at home anywhere else. Gloria will grow here just like her mother did. I have employed a Nanny for her. She is none other than the woman who saved us both the next day. She lives in our outhouse.

Affectionately yours
Leonard Ashworth

***

Whenever Gloria started the story, "Shyllong the beautiful boy was stillborn to a virgin mother Lir in the village near Bisi," Cecil would listen wide-eyed and slightly open mouthed, but as she grew she started asking, "Is Khasi community really matriarchal?" During her pre-teens one day she asked, "Is it still matriarchal?" Gloria had said, "Yes my Cecil darling, in our Shillong women power rules!"

"Shyllong means 'one who grows naturally'. Now, Cecil, don't ask me if we all grow unnaturally. Lir was awakened at midnight by the noise of a large crowd. As she opened the door, a tall, handsome youth stepped forward and said, "Mother, I am the baby you buried in the garden. Don't be afraid you are my earthly mother and I came so that all our people can prosper and live happily. Now, I shall instruct uncles, kith, and kin on how to perform ceremonies. Since then, he has been the presiding deity of Shillong."

Gloria stopped telling her that tale when Cecil started asking, "How can a virgin have a baby?" And when Cecil reached her teens, when Gloria tried to convince, "If you believe in what father Steven tells you about Jesus on Sunday classes, then why can't you believe this?"

"When did I ever say I believed what he said?" Cecil had said with a rebellious expression, and that's when Gloria had stopped telling her the mythological and folk stories of the known and unknown lands she grew up listening from her Nanny.

Staring intently at the globe on her table when Cecil asked one day, "How is it that my dad and your dad were so similar in abandoning their wife and child?" Gloria tried to explain that she and her mother had refused to leave for England, but Cecil was never ready to buy that. As Cecil grew older, she asked the same question but in several different ways, more and more cynically and Gloria learned to keep her mouth shut.

***

'Ten Commandments' is screened after the exams are over and the teachers are busy correcting piles and piles of answer sheets. Most of the girls are disinterested in the movie.

"*Birakthikara*!" someone sulks behind sister's back. "Who is talking in Assamese?" A few girls laugh when Madhumitha stands up and tells politely, "That's Bengali, Sister."

"Have you all forgotten what Sister Thomas said during the assembly on Monday morning? You will be fined if you talk in any language other than English. Madhumitha, you will note down the name of those who talk, and also those who talk in any tongue other than English." She nods with an uneasy expression and seats herself back.

"Tere mere bheech me kysaa hai he bandhan .. ," someone hums the Hindi hit film number by a new male playback singer.

Sister Isabel turns to check who hummed it. She calls out aloud with an irritation. "Don't sing or hum, watch the movie." She goes on repeating the same patiently every a few minutes, but every time after seconds of silence, the girls continue to ignore the Ten Commandments and start indulging in their secret gossips.

"Doesn't Moses's character resemble that of Karna of Mahabharata?" Madhumitha asks feebly, but seriously with her eyes on the screen. "Not only were both infants set adrift by their mothers in baskets but have their mothers' wrapped clothes that led them to their mothers later on in their lives."

"Are you into some comparative study?" the girls laugh.

"My stomach is pleading. Hope school canteen has vegetable chops left. I don't want to end up eating the potato chops."

"There would have been pin drop silence now if 'Ek Duuje Ke Liye' was screened," a couple of girls whisper without getting caught.

Suddenly Sister is not to be seen. The students look around and get all smiling and happy to talk freely and loudly. When they see her return with a stainless steel drum half full of cold water, their chattering stops abruptly. Sister has a small tumbler in her hand. No one can guess what she is up to. Certainly not for drinking, they think.

After a few minutes of silence when the girls restart talking, Sister scoops a tumbler full of icy cold water from the drum and splashes in the direction of the chattering. Getting wet mostly on their cardigans, the girls yell and scream.

At the moment, Mother Cecil unexpectedly appears. She stands with a wave of stern anger in her face with both her hands on her waist. Sister Isabel hesitates a moment and keeps the tumbler on the drum and leaves the hall. "I was only following Sister Thomas's instruction, trying my best to get the girls to watch the film," she murmurs as she passes Mother.

"Is that the way she recommended?" Mother hisses under her breath pointing to the drum. "That's cruelty if you would like to know," she mumbles in a low volume. The girls start watching the movie silently.

***

30 December 1980

Dear diary, it's almost a year since I visited you. You must be wondering, "Why hasn't Cecil touched me so long." My fingers have recovered, and it's a great feeling to be able to write again. I want to write all those flashes in my mind today.

Other parts of my shoulders and head escaped with many bruises. Trying to guard my head against their aimless and erratic whackings, I had severely injured my fingers, and worse were those of my right hands, fractured beyond repair. They are barely functional, but no more improvement expected, I understand.

Memories remain, magically, and those keep me amused like a child. Interestingly, Shillong day coincides with my birthday. I still remember fourteen years ago when we celebrated 100 years of Shillong. The Malki Fete lingers in my memories when Sister Thomas went 'Sambar' hunting more than twice with two empty bottles to the stall that sold 'Masala dosas.' She was taken back to her South Indian native town just with its aroma, she had said. Oh how she shed tears of joy at the dining table relishing the gravy with the brown rice! We were all so fascinated by her happiness.

The rock music bands have increased so much these days in Shillong that it's never easy to distinguish amateur bands from the professional ones. The new Hindi movie Qurbani is occupying the minds of our youth in recent months. The songs are heard everywhere. Bijou cinema is houseful every show I hear.

During the riots here in Shillong last October those who were not tribals were targeted. A group surrounded me while I was walking along the Laitumkhra Road towards our convent. As they continued to beat me calling 'foreigner,' I was extremely puzzled. Even mama was a complete Shillong girl, who has never been to England. We are all locals, but it's a pity our skin speaks differently.

It's bizarre that only this globe on my table remains of my lineage, except of course our 'Shillong.' It was not anymore the like when I grew up. I hope the name Hopkinson Road is retained in the unplanned changes the city is going through. The golf links, referred to as Glenn Eagles of the East are dwindling in size due to building constructions. Concrete structures and increasing vehicle pollution are drastically changing climatic conditions. The dense greenish atmosphere at our convent is also not spared. Management could try and do more to preserve as much as possible, but it's a pity it has other interests.

I was fortunate to have been saved by an Assamese couple who drove that way. If not for them, I would have died on the road the same day. I was partially unconscious when I heard feebly the lady saying, "Oh my God! Aren't you the son of our domestic helper? You supposed to be studying for your final year exams! Hop in, I can't leave you here. Your mother is going to be heart-broken," Are the ancient inter-tribal battles forgotten over the centuries being revived, I wondered in my unconscious state as they drove me to the hospital.

***

My mother is a feminist

Walking near the hawker center along Bangkit road, I thought to myself, very soon I might end up committing suicide. A young Malay girl, shocked, stared at my face as she swiftly passed by. That's when I realized that I had spoken the words aloud.

I reached the public phone. Sally picked at the second ring. A little hesitantly she asked, "Who is this please?" a little intrigued but in a sweet, song-like tone.

When I said, "Dewei," she became silent for a few seconds. I could hear her soft breath on the other side, or so I imagined.

When I asked her, "Why did you block my number, Sally?" my stomach growled at the aroma that floated from the chicken rice stall at the back, and I involuntarily turned to look. The elderly folks' group seated there playing Chinese Checkers laughed boisterously, and I had to raise my voice to say, "I sent you a friend request on Facebook and you rejected that as well. Can't you at least accept that?"

"I've told you many times not to disturb me. Don't you understand English?" Sally hissed harshly. I was surprised at the sudden sternness in her voice.

"All I want is your friendship. Please, Sally!"

"But I don't want your friendship. Can't you understand that? Don't you have friends of your age?"

"I left them all because I fought with them. These days, my buddies avoid me, ridicule me and all because of you." I tried to talk fast, but she wouldn't listen.

"Don't be stupid lah. I have never seen such dumb of a boy. Did I tell you to leave them? Boy, grow up and complete your final year," she coaxed me and cut the connection off abruptly.

Slamming the phone in its place, I uttered, "Bitch!" and quickly looked around to see if anyone had heard.

I was reminded of the invitation that Han had sent me in the WhatsApp group a couple of weeks after that unfortunate night. They were gathering to chill out at the Sentosa resort.

I never expected it to turn out the way it turned to be. I never thought they would go that extent. Ravi had left earlier, but Han knew everything because he was with me that night. However, I didn't expect him to spill the bean.

Everyone was joking and ridiculing me. "You are welcome to bring along your girlfriends. Dewei can invite his cocotte." If my friend Ravi had not stopped me, I would have indeed gone over to Han's house to kill him. I was furious.

***

Perspiring, I walked frantically. I remembered having seen a public phone in the basement of Bukit Panjang Plaza. Only upon reaching there did I realize that I had no more of the twenty cent coins in my pocket. Hurriedly I went to buy a small coke at McDonald's, to get some coins. Upon reaching there, I craved for a double cheese but decided to buy it after calling Sally.

For the first time, I realized the increase in my recent appetite.

"Nee Hau."

"Sally, please add me back in WhatsApp," I pleaded, the moment I heard her.

"You again?"

"I can't get over you, Sally. Nor can I concentrate on anything. Are you afraid your earnings might be affected?"

"Ya, so? So what if I fear that my income will drop? I need to expand my circle of men. Your kind of emotional attachment can only pull me down, and I know it very well," she yelled. "Call my new agent if you want my service."

"What kind of a profession is this, with zero morals?" I tried to provoke her.

"Were you all clean with morals that night? Don't start spitting the words you drank from your mama, okay?"

"I'll kill myself, and you will be the reason for that and I will write that down clearly."

"Don't call me again. Otherwise, I will report you to the police."

"Okay lah, go ahead and report and let your family know of the life you are leading."

"Shut up. How does that bother you?" Sally shouted and cut the line.

Reaching home, I texted mother, "Are you back tonight?"

"No, tomorrow night, why?" she replied, with a wide smiley.

Wondering why she couldn't return now that all the guests of the funeral gathering would have left, I typed instead, "I'm damn ravenous."

***

I rubbed my eyes as I came into the living room.

"I'm not myself, ma," I said.

The sight of her brought about aggressive war with the acids in my stomach.

"Maybe your final year result next week is bothering you," mother said, as she continued to keep her eyes on the television screen.

Her unopened travel bag lay in on the corner of the living room near the front door.

Cloudy and gloomy, it was ready to rain. The sky is in the same mood as I am, I thought.

"I don't care about the results. I hear voices telling me to commit suicide."

"Voices? Bullshit! You are just too tired," she stretched her hand to touch my forehead. I pulled myself backward. She touched me with her four fingers anyway. "You don't have a fever."

"Come on. You have been googling too much, I guess," she tried to laugh. "I think I will walk to the wet market later. Want to join me? We could have breakfast on our way back. Then I can cook lunch."

The acids in my stomach were creating havoc. I reached for the bread loaf. "Aren't you cooking?" Hurriedly I swallowed the slice I had munched. "I think I have schizophrenia."

"I hear voices telling me I don't deserve to live in this world, and lately I talk loudly to myself, and that's been increasing in the past few days."

She reminded me of my recent text messages and expressed her concern all over again. When she started lecturing me on the importance of strengthening one's mind, staring at her angrily, I showed her my palm, gesturing her to stop.

"It's not even nine yet, why don't you try sleeping off your stress now that you have all the time and luxury?"

"So, you think I am imagining?" I made a serious face. "Make me some soup noodles now, and I am ready to come with you to the market."

"Try applying for some internship, to keep yourself busy."

"I need to tell you something," I yelled as I switched off the TV. "And you must promise me that you will die with this secret of mine."

"Dewei, I want to watch that. It's the final presidential," she said. Seeing her smilingly go for the remote, I pounced to grab it in a flash and threw it towards my bedroom.

Shouting disproportionately, "To hell with the US and your Hillary!"

"What's it this time?" she turned solemn. "Are you very hungry?"

"When am I not very hungry?"

"Don't shout at me as if I am the cause. Maybe blame it all on your hormones."

"I am frustrated at my hunger, ma. I wish I could do something about this constant feeling of starving."

"Fought with Han?"

"No. Every night, I dream of a woman, get disturbed and I haven't been sleeping properly for several weeks. A few days back, after midnight, I went up to the thirty- first storey, only to hurriedly return home in seconds," I said, bringing down the volume of my voice.

"Don't be so stupid, lah! I think you need a good break." She got up to go to the kitchen. "Is it your ex?" She placed the Danish pot with the half-filled water on the stove.

I followed her into the kitchen. "No, a woman in her late thirties."

Mother turned to the fridge and took out the ingredients one by one. Taking out the frozen peas from the freezer, she started to chop the onions, carrot, beans, garlic and, mushrooms on the cutting board.

"Oh, just a dream!" she said.

I watched her stir-fry the onions and toss the cut vegetable in a separate pan and add them to the pot that boiled the noodles to finish off with a dash of salt and some pepper.

"It's the same woman every time. And she is a whore."

"What nonsense?" Mother's expression terrified me.

Pretending to be calm I said, "Yes."

"You mean...?" With the ladle held abruptly half-way, she stopped stirring.

"It happened last month. And now,... now don't get emotional. I beg of you, please, ma," I sat adjacent to her.

Open-mouthed, Mother stared at me in complete shock. Her eyes, frozen, welled quickly like an urban flash-flood. She switched off the stove and hurried to seat herself back on the single sofa.

"Fifteen years older than you?" she managed a mundane question as if trying to conceal her hurt.

"Fourteen. But does that matter?"

"Precisely. Only your inappropriate indulgence shocks me."

"But, she is responsible for the state I am in," I said, as she sat in the next single-seater.

"What do you mean?" her voice held a little irritation and a lot of anger.

"After that incident, I felt so much wanted, so much cared, so much that I am unable to get over her," I cried despondently. The big drops of my tears shocked mother just as they did me. I never knew I could weep like that.

"But you just said she ruined you, Dewei. And stop crying like a child," Mother said, gritting her teeth.

"She has completely shattered me." I wiped my tears.

"Did she come to our doorstep to drag you?" she piqued.

"How is she able to do this kind of a job hiding from her family, especially her nineteen-year-old daughter?"

"That's none of our business."

"Aren't you against her ways?"

"Is she my sister or a cousin? Anyway, that's her profession, and we don't know her journey. Its none of our business, Dawei."

"But she screwed your son's life! How can you even side with her? How could you talk in favour of her?"

"I am not favouring her."

"You are siding with her."

"Okay, let me ask you something. Did that woman cross your path? Only you crossed hers. I have nothing against her."

"The guys gave me too many that day," I said, to justify myself.

"If you can't handle it, then why drink?"

"It was Ravi's birthday ma. We reached there late. She was assigned to entertain our group. I remember thinking about how I ended up in that room when I woke up there the next morning."

"From that day you felt 'wanted' and 'cared'?" Her eyes welled once again. "Not in our family, Dewei."

"I keep thinking of her."

"And that's called 'wanted' in your vocabulary?"

"I think I love her very much."

"Nonsense! Aren't you old enough to know that she would do the same to hundreds of guys and they all know that's her profession and she is not for real? You are almost twenty-three, Dewei, please." She was wiping away at her cheeks.

"..."

"That's instant gratification, or may be mere lust. You are misnaming your feelings and your needs."

"I just can't get over her. But why do you keep siding with her, ma?"

"I am not siding with her. It's just that I am angry when you say she ruined your life."

"A typical feminist! That's what you are. My life is gone, and you don't sympathize with me at all."

"I don't think your life is ruined. That's your imagination."

"Ravi says she must have done something to me like black magic."

"Rubbish," she said sternly. "Okay, let's come back to you. I think you should see a doctor, a psychiatrist. Let him decide on the diagnosis. Let's go tomorrow to get a referral."

When I hurried to say, "No, I will go alone, on my own," mother said, "Okay, then please go as soon as possible."

"Slut!" I murmured as I checked my WhatsApp.

"And you?" Full of annoyance, she looked up at me.

"Do you think she can sleep well?" I tried to digress as I reached for my wallet on the TV console.

"How does that bother you?" Mother said, glaring at me.

"I was thinking with that kind of earning…" I said as I checked the contents of my wallet involuntarily.

"Did she dope your drink that day?"

"No, I don't think so."

"Then? I am searching for the values that Dad and I inculcated in you since young. Ironically, your grandfather gave you such a nice name, 'Dewei,' meaning' highly noble.'"

"I know Grandfather gave me that name, but…are you judging me now?"

"I am not just your friend but also your mother, and you almost always forget that, rather conveniently."

"Are you disappointed with me?" I asked her.

"Didn't you hide it from me only because I would be?"

"You are not a man, ma, so you won't know what I am going through," I said, trying to win over at least little of her sympathy.

"You will start feeling some peace only if you take it all on yourself and think hard. Stop finding external reasons to blame her and many justifications for your actions."

She went to the kitchen to pour the soup noodles in the bowl. I switched on the fan as I sat at the table. "Oh, how I yearned for this. Can I eat it? Sorry, I am not waiting for you. When is Dad returning?"

"Next Wednesday? He told me to tell you to go to Johor this weekend."

"But why so long?" I asked while I looked at my mobile.

Ravi had texted, "Will you join me for breakfast? Usual place in ten minutes?"

I typed, "Yes."

Mother glared at me. "She is his only sister, who was almost his mother, and she has passed away."

I left in a hurry. Mother's voice followed me, "You said you would come with me to the wet market."

"Sorry, I am going for breakfast with Ravi."

"And what was that?" She pointed at the big bowl on the table.

I shrugged my shoulders and waved my hand as I ran down.

***

When I came out of the consultation room, Ravi looked instantly up at my face, and I said, "It's depression, he says."

Looking around, Ravi said, "I told you." He suppressed his laughter, as his face displaying a slight self-pride.

"You respond like it's only the common flu, not dengue."

"These days depression is like a common cold. Did you tell the doctor everything?"

"Ya lah," I said a little impatiently.

"You sound unhappy because it's not some fancy name you had imagined, but just a simple depression?"

We walked towards the pharmacy. "I have to try somehow to get Sally's daughter's phone number. Her old agent is hopeless."

"And what's that for?" Ravi looked at me.

"To tell on her."

"Why so evil? This odious Dewei is new for me. What do you achieve by that?"

I said, "Doesn't she feel guilty? Doesn't she have any shame? Does she even know what will happen if her daughter knows?"

"Come on, and you think her family will believe you? Why so keen on her friendship anyway? Hey, I've been thinking of asking you something. Did you by any chance leave any of your personal belongings in her place?"

"No, why?"

"The guys also said something to me that day, something like she has an air of black magic. These women do all that to keep their business thriving. Have you heard of Nam Man Prai Oil from Thailand?"

"No lah, definitely not across the sea into Singapore. They say it loses its effect if taken across the sea. And it's damn expensive."

"But there are ways to bring it. They tie the green, red, white, black and yellow strings to the bottle or put the bottle in a bag and tie the bag with those strings, and then the effect remains they say but it's not easy to get a genuine product, I heard."

"Hey, shall we go for a bite?" I asked instead, to which

Ravi replied, "WHAT?!? thought we had a heavy lunch before coming to the clinic."

"Did we?" I laughed at his serious face when he said, "My stomach is so full that I can't have dinner. And you ate double the amount, remember?"

"Whether you believe it or not, I am famished."

"You have a voracious appetite. And…"

"I am equally voracious about it." I held him by the shoulder.

"Any quantity is not enough for me."

"Were you born a glutton? Ha, ha. Jokes apart, did you tell the doctor about your abnormal hunger?"

I nodded yes. "And hey, Ravi, I remember smelling something horrid and unpleasant before I left her place at dawn."

"You did? Then it's certainly corpse oil." Aghast, Ravi halted, staring at me. "Nam Man Prai Oil!"

Suddenly, I realised I had never been that hungry ever before. Before the night I spent with her.

***

Am I a jar?

Whatsapp:

Barbara: I got your number from your cousin. Do you remember we met at the bar the other day?

Natasha: Barbara?

As they entered, Granny looked at Natasha like she was observing an alien from another planet. "Why has she cut her hair so close like a boy?" she asked with a seriousness looking at her Mother. "And why a silver earring only in one ear?"

Natasha glared fiercely at her mother. "This is why I was reluctant to come," her eyes with impertinence seemed to yell. Not opening her mouth, her mother turned to look at her father, who tried his best to be supportive.

"Ma, how are your knees now?" he asked.

But Granny didn't seem to listen to him. She went on to ask, "I remember she had such long flowing, beautiful lustrous hair last time when I visited you."

"Ma, please ignore her, will you? I can't wait to taste your green bean soup, my favourite."

"Is this money plant?" Shan asked Granny. Excited at his question, she said, "It's called by many names," as she kept glowering on Natasha. "When is that boy coming back? Timothy! A gem of a boy! Will he like this drastic change of hers?" she asked Natasha's mother who stood nearby.

Shaking her head in hopelessness, Granny turned back to her plants. "They remain green even when kept in the dark or indoors," she explained smiling at Shan.

"You came here when you were much younger."

Shan nodded. "*Jiejie*?"

"Oh, your sister used to visit me before, but not anymore. Jurong has become a neighbouring country for her."

"We are off on different days and also because of Caesar, we are unable to leave home ma. Our neighbour is helping us to look after him only for today," Natasha's mother tried but could not catch Granny's attention.

Using her pruning shears with a fluid movement, Granny said to Shan, "It grows so fast, needs to be trimmed regularly." Ganny's fingers, though a little crooked because of arthritis were swift and steady.

"Oh! It looks a little different but nice, I mean the leaves with those yellowish streaks and patches," Shan said widening his eyes.

"There are a few varieties with minute differences. It's strong in tackling formaldehyde."

"Is it?"

"Do you know what formaldehyde is?"

"An organic compound also called methanol."

"Oh, you do seem to know!"

"I learnt that in chemistry. I'm in sec two now," Shan said with a slight pride.

"Devil's ivy purifies the air naturally. It should not be kept in direct sun. It is sensitive to draughts. Little water but even dampness should suffice. Spraying water like this, once a day, helps."

At the dining table, Granny kept looking at Natasha but didn't utter a word. After dinner, when they were about to leave, she asked, "Why don't you both do something as parents? People will take us to be indecorous. How can we have this girl like this at the gathering next month?" asked Granny with a dramatic look of dismay. Her concern focused on her seventieth birthday banquet planned for next month.

Increased humidity announced the expected night rains.

"Don't worry. I won't embarrass you all with my presence," Natasha said as she exited the apartment in a flash towards the lift. The other three followed her. Shan waved to Granny.

On their way back to Tampines, in the car, her mother said, "Granny told me to tell you to keep away from those 'unnatural' people. She means well."

"What does she know about my friends?"

"Keep your voice down, Natasha," Father said softly but strictly.

"I am born that way."

"Never. That stupid girlfriend of yours is insinuating you," Mother said sternly. Shan watched them for a few minutes like he was watching a drama and later diverted his attention to his video game.

"Guys don't treat gals properly, and so our number will increase," she announced.

Looking at Shan in the rearview mirror, "Hush," Mother said sternly.

***

Whatsapp:

Barbara: I heard you go to all the places you went with that guy.
Natasha: Ya, I miss him, but I am slowly getting over.
Barbara: Sorry, I was not ridiculing you.

Natasha's mother looked tired. Having just come back from work, she was irritated, a little more than usual. The rains were gradually reducing.

Seeing Natasha dressed and ready to go out, she asked in a sulky voice, "I thought you were off today. Where are you going?" No answer. "With whom?" No answer. "Then it is definitely with that girl."

"Ya, so?" Natasha retorted.

"Did I ever ask you all these when you used to date Timothy?"

"You did but a little differently, and only I can remember them all, okay?" Natasha said vehemently.

"But I never felt uneasy back then. Anyway, where are you going now?" Mother gathered strength to raise her voice.

"To a movie. Does that hurt you?"

"Look at your cousin, so modern and trendy, but she does not dress like you."

"I am not a twelve-year-old, okay? Why do you compare us?"

"I certainly don't mean to."

"But you are. There is nothing anymore like dressing like a boy or dressing like a girl. And clothing is something very personal not to do with what others feel or like, okay?"

"Imagine, Shan, starting to wear skirts at your age."

"What if he does? Stop talking like a cavewoman."

"You are becoming more and more stupid than I had ever imagined. Don't go out with that girl, Natasha."

"What the f...? Why are you biased against her? You never said anything when I went shopping with your niece."

"Annie is not like her. I will tell your dad if you go out with her."

"You think I am scared of him?"

"Our relatives are talking behind our backs."

"What are they talking?"

"That you are a.."

"Ya, I am one. Let them think all they want."

"But I don't want you to be one Natasha, please."

"I can't be what you want me to be. I am almost twenty-three. You are controlling me too much, and I don't like that."

"Look at your hair sticking out like straws and sticks! Granny always complains that I give you too much freedom."

"Do you even know the meaning of freedom?" she gave a burst of sarcastic laughter, looking hard into her mother's face. "Hm,.. of late, you choose to have these sessions when Shan is not at home. You are becoming cleverer ma."

Ignoring her mother's glare, Natasha stroked Caesar before walking swiftly out towards the lift. Jumping and barking, he tried to follow her.

***

Whatsapp:

Barbara: Guys are nothing but trouble. Stay over at my place for a few days. I will show you how fast you will forget him. I know you are new. Don't worry only Bambi for the first few days. We won't rush.

The tables indoors had been pushed to the side, the volume of the music had gone up, and the lights had gone wild, Natasha remembered. One of her distant friends had pulled her along to that bar. The girls had gotten on the makeshift dance floor. The change in the ambiance in 'Rooftop of Bar Empire' had seemed to invite everyone to try free movements.

"Try any, the wide choice of Martini menu is good here," Barbara had recommended handing the menu to her Caucasian friend. "And they have a few originals concocted by the owners themselves."

"I visited 'Croc Rock.' With a mature crowd of young and working professional women, it was not bad."

"Of course, being the oldest and longest-running les pub. And they have strictly English music. That's one thing I like about that place."

"I heard the weekdays are the best there for those who love to sing. They say it's quiet and you mostly won't have to fight for the karaoke mike."

"Ya, I've been there once."

Essaying a broad smile, bubbly looking Barbara had come near, "You are damn attractively curvy." Natasha had just smiled. "Femme, I suppose," she had whispered into her ears. Natasha had shaken her head in a fast denial, which Barbara had failed to notice. "As you can see I'm butch. How often do you come here?" She had turned back to ask.

Natasha had forced another smile. She wished her not to think that that was her first time there. Perhaps the last time, she'd thought then as she was not too comfortable that evening.

"I guess you like it here for the same reason as mine. Strictly no men allowed. Just the way I love it."

The blonde friend of Barbara had said with an angry face, "Idiots, the guys assume because I am a femme, they can flirt with me and that I would surely sleep with them." Natasha had continued to look at her face with astonishment but gave the same old smile when Barbara had asked, "Are you okay?"

Suddenly there was a commotion. Two girls, with livid expressions, had pounced on each other pulling each other's hairs. "Don't worry, they are friends, fighting over a girl." They'd screamed vulgarities at each other. "Could you both please go out and fight," the bar owner had come near to tell them politely. Instantly they'd stopped the fight.

"A desperation number I suppose," her friend had said to Barbara. Not understanding, Natasha had looked blank.

Barbara had walked that night with Natasha to catch the last train at City Hall. "Can I touch your long hair just once?" she had asked eagerly, and Natasha nodded. Barbara touched hair from the scalp to the tip.

"The night is still beautiful," she had said before boarding the train in the opposite direction. Natasha remembered Barbara having waved broadly at her as the train moved.

***

Whatsapp:

Natasha: I like Susan a lot. She seems to be with a different girl every time. I have been watching her for months from afar. She is elegant and very soft spoken. Please introduce me to her. I want to be her steady. Please help me with this.

Barbara: What about me then?

Natasha: Sorry, but I thought.

Barbara: Don't worry, I was only joking. Relax. But you might have to start concealing your curves. You might have to wear sports bra to flatten, will you?

Natasha's mother was not even half an hour into her sleep when her mobile rang. Startled, she jumped to grab it. Pressing to her ears, she mumbled, "Hello."

"Ma, can you come and pick me up?" Natasha asked falteringly.

"Where are you?"

"At the bar, lah. Don't you know where I work?" she shouted with impudence as if she was with a close friend. Mother had no choice but to let go of the sleep she was trying hard to hold. "I'm damn sleepy, Natasha. And I hate to come to that place. Why don't you take a cab back?"

"Not getting taxi, ma. Tried calling many times," she said unclearly.

"Why is your voice so slurry? Are you alone?" she yawned.

"Why do you always ask strings of questions? Is there a manufacturing defect in you?" Natasha yelled again.

"Did you drink?"

"I didn't want to, but they forced me to," she mellowed slightly. "But it was fun," she ended with a jump in her voice.

Looking at the back of her husband facing the other side, deep asleep, Natasha's mother was tempted to wake him up but decided against it.

"Okay, I'll come now. Stay right there." She hurriedly brushed her hair that looked a skein before leaving.

"This girl is nothing but trouble," she mumbled as she took the car key.

On the way, during the drive back home from China town, Mother said, "Quit this stupid job, Natasha."

"I won't," she said with a slight laugh as she slowly reclined on the rear seat.

"You have dark circles, and you look totally drained. Blame it all on this night job."

".."

"Take up some office job."

"I hate office jobs. That's why I left my previous one."

"Aren't you paid only five dollars an hour?"

"When I am okay with it, how does that bother you?"

"Try to complete your poly at least, Natasha."

"How many times should I tell you that I've no interest in studies?"

"You can do a short course entirely new," piqued mother.

"But, I don't have the money."

"I will tell dad. He will sponsor."

"No, don't tell him," she raised her voice suddenly.

"Why?"

"I already wasted a year of the fees in poly, haven't I?"

"It's okay. I will tell him."

"You said I wasted the fee, last year when dad was really considering options of sending me to Australia. You convinced him that I would waste more money, didn't you?"

"Do a course in Singapore. It won't be too expensive."

"No, I still remember and it makes me feel guilty…I hate that…" "Start saving, at least. You can spend on your fees. I thought you wanted to go to Paris to do a course in fashion designing."

"It's okay if I don't go," she said in a desultory tone.

"Isn't the 50 dollars weekly allowance enough for you? Why work for such low wages?"

"I want more money for shopping and movies. I wish to live, okay? Not just keep planning and dreaming the future with no real action, like you all." Natasha didn't respond after that when her mother tried to ask something. Upon reaching the car park, Natasha had to be shaken.

She dragged herself slowly when Mother helped her to be steady as if she was maneuvering a cupboard.

Seeing her opening her eyes while in the lift mother said, "Why don't you have some real ambition in life?"

"I will kill myself very soon if you continue to lecture me like this."

Caesar started barking in the room when they exited the lift. Natasha went straight to him and let him pounce on her. "Okay okay, Caesar boy. Let me go to sleep." And only after a few minutes of playing with him she went to her room to sleep.

***

Whatsapp:

Barbara: But Susan does not like femmes. You need to become a butch first if you really want to impress her, will you? You are such a good girl, I don't know if you can change in the first place. You will have to cut off your hair, colour it trendy with spikes. And of course, your wardrobe will need a total replacement.

Natasha: Okay. I will crop my hair today itself. Please help with clothes shopping.

Caesar kept barking and barking the moment Raj was at their door. Scared, he couldn't relax until Caesar was locked away in the room. "Today is only the second day he saw you. He will get used to you soon," Natasha's mother said smilingly. "And you to him."

Just when Raj entered, he was stunned for a second. Natasha was crossing the living room with a newspaper in her hand. "Is she a les,..?" he swallowed his words and managed to utter, "Sorry aunty," and rushed into the study.

Looking at his expression, Natasha ran into her room.

In the study, Raj asked Shan, "Is Caesar a mixed breed?"

"Jack Russel Terrier."

"Although I get petrified of dogs, I love watching them from far," Raj chirped. "My friend in Bangkok has one; he says he is a Shih Tzu."

"Lion dog."

"Ya, any difficulties in Mensuration?"

"Can't we have the value of π rounded off to 3 universally? Half of my problems would vanish."

Raj laughed loudly and said, "We can't have those our way. Let's go the regular way."

***

In the evening, Natasha's mother invited Anitha for a chat at the coffee shop. "Did your son share anything with you, Anitha?"

"No, why?" she suddenly became concerned.

"Raj almost asked if Natasha was a Les."

"Oh my God! Crude though, I'm sure it was an innocuous question. Nevertheless, I apologise on his behalf."

"No, I'm not offended."

"Okay, then what's bothering you, then?"

"She has peculiar hair spikes and clothing."

"That need not indicate anything in particular. As you know, I too have a closely cropped hair."

"Yours is still very much like a woman's hair, Anitha. Natasha colours her hair orange sometimes parrot green."

"What?" Anitha exclaimed spontaneously.

"You haven't seen her recently. A couple of months back, I asked her straight on her, are you a lesbian?"

"So blatantly?" Anitha widened her eyes.

"Why beat around? You know, I'm too straight forward."

"You could have slowly come to the point."

"That's beyond the point. She screamed at me. Why do you ask all these?" I asked her calmly why she had discarded all her beautiful clothes. She shouted, it's her wish and screamed at me not to interfere in her affairs. She called me "an old fashioned hag."

***

Whatsapp:

Barbara: We will go to the boutique I had mentioned before. You will like the particular variety of jeans, tees, bags and essential accessories of Freitag, Tretorn, GSUS. We will be spoilt for choice.

Natasha had watched as Barbara joined in the conversation among the group of her friends from Australia. "The funniest part is that many think that men haters are all lesbians or all lesbians turn out to be men-haters." There was a group nearby roaring with laughter at some bawdy jokes. "*Ivalukku vilakki sonnathaan puriyumaam.* [24]"

"The moment you judge a person and put her in a box as if labeling a jar in your kitchen, the problem begins," the tall and slim young genial woman from Western Australia had begun with astuteness, seriously looking around everyone's face. "When people stop understanding something or someone, they conveniently start to 'label' them. They don't need any effort there."

"Don't we have smaller labels between us?" Barbara giggled.

"A point to ponder," the blonde had agreed. "Last weekend, my girlfriend and I were given such a hard time at the bar,"

Barbara's friend Alya asked instantly. "*Apa yang berlaku*? [25]"

"I just wanted to ask them, because we both are born this way, are we posing as threats to others?"

"I've heard many such stories," Barbara had proudly thrown her plump hands up in the air.

"Just because we're both femmes, they think we were different in the crowd. They are okay if either of us is a butch."

---

24 Ivalukku vilakki sonnathaan puriyumaam – (In Tamil) Everything needs to be explained elaborately for her to understand.

25 Apa yang berlaku?" – (In Malay) What happened?

"Oh!" Barbara with her hand around Natasha's waist had sipped her red wine and as if to check if she were listening, she'd looked at her face.

"It was entirely a discovery for me. It's not like this back home in our place. I've been thinking oh my god, how queer human minds can be? Even the smallest of an issue does not get a panoptic view of such people."

"And I thought this city is becoming a little liberal," Barbara had added.

"It's not just about being liberal or not liberal. The core of a society always seeps through everywhere, as my good friend had rightly put. Just because a person is unique, everyone thinks they have all the right to judge her. They are tuned to see only the differences, which is still acceptable. What I can't stand is when they create prejudice against those differences."

"You might have heard, Pink Dot is a new group that holds an annual gathering, you should join us," Barbara had invited.

"I shall try," she'd said with a polite smile. "I need to check my calendar."

Barbara handed her a name card, "It's a cozy environment in the heart of Orchard Rd. You are sure to feel rejuvenated and relaxed. It's my friend who runs it. Most sought after place. You must see to believe it. Prior booking is needed. I can help you with that. They have a professional and friendly male therapist in that spa."

"I'll consider. Coming back to the topic, I've got a Les friend here struggling to keep her orientation a secret, so it's even harder for her. The struggle begins from within. And if she wants to be open about her preferences outside of her close friend's circles, she can expect all prejudice, hostility, and stares."

"Some women can't tell the word lesbian even when their heads and mouths are so full of it. I know a few."

—

Whatsapp:

Barbara: Don't thank me too fast. It's not easy to impress Susan, a staunch lipstick les. Remember, I had warned you? You'll need to change the way you speak, your body language, etc. Try all possible ways. Good luck!

Natasha was having her breakfast. "I am going to work in the casino," she said when her mother walked past her into the kitchen.

"Why suddenly?"

"I'm not asking your opinion or permission but just telling you my decision," Natasha said.

"Night shift?"

"What a stupid question!"

"Don't take the job if it is night shift."

"I get good pay. And I love the nightlife. What else can I ask for? I am joining."

"Natasha, please think of your future, like your marriage."

"Future? Marriage?" Natasha roared with a peal of loud, bitter laughter. "I can choose to be a bisexual lesbian if that can help you. But I will announce it to the boy you might stubbornly introduce to me. Also to his family."

Ignoring her sarcasm, mother said, "Timothy might return very soon."

"To hell with your Timothy! Anyway, who is waiting for him?"

"Don't shout, Natasha. Granny is sleeping. She is tired after last night's event."

"I will leave home if you keep pestering me."

"That day you did not go to the movie. Annie said she saw you both hand in hand in Orchard area."

With sarcasm all over her face, Natasha clapped her hands. "Oh, so you have informers?"

"Is she also joining the casino?"

"Ya, we both are joining. Any objection?"

"So you don't mind letting her control you." Her mother shook Natasha holding her shoulders with both her hands.

"You are going to wake her up now."

"Please stop letting her control you so much. It might go beyond correction."

"I am not your slave or pet."

"You talk as if I am your enemy."

"Were you ever a friend to me? Never. None of you were there when I had my lows. Only she was with me all along."

"You are purposely digressing."

"I don't want to be late for my interview. Bye," Natasha rushed to the shoe rack.

"Wait till dad comes home."

"He won't object, you are the,.."

"He must be on the way. I will text him," she reached for her mobile.

"No need. I will talk to him on my way."

"Quit this job and leave that girl."

"I like both and am not leaving both. Don't keep waylaying me. I won't talk with anyone anymore in this house."

"So you want to be a man?"

"A butch does not want to become a man. She is a woman, and she knows it. Similarly, a femme guy does not want to become a woman. He remains a man, and he is aware of it. Get these straight first in your stupid head," Natasha said pointing her index finger at her. Mother just stared at her. "How many of you people understand these?"

—

Father called Natasha's name the moment he entered the house back from work, but his call did not have the anxiety or anger that it usually echoed after her mother feeds him with the day's arguments or happenings. His voice only had anguish and a subtle concern, Natasha felt. Almost ready to leave for work, Natasha came out, "Pa, I need to leave for work," She looked at him questioningly.

"I'll drop you today," he turned to walk when Natasha said with a curious look, "I still have time. You can wash and change if you want." She wondered what was bothering him.

"Get me some tea, will you?" he asked as he sat at the dining table. "Ma," she was about to call when her father said, "Don't call her."

Looking at his forehead with lines of thought, she went into the kitchen to bring him his tea. When father sipped, she went to her room to collect her bag and things. She wondered why he was unusually preoccupied.

When she was back, he was ready near the lift. They were silent as they reached the car park. She took the front seat. Wearing her belt, she looked to her right at her father looking straight ahead as he started the ignition.

Driving on the road, "How's your new job?" he asked her.

"So far so good," she said. "Pa, is anything bothering you?"

"No, but I had to share something with you."

"Go ahead," she said as she took out her mobile to check her messages when her father said, "Not now, please. I need to talk."

"Okay," she put it away into her bag.

"I hardly get to see you these days, Natasha. You leave before I reach, and in the morning I get to see only your sleeping face before I leave, but your mother has been updating me."

Natasha didn't say anything. She just looked at his face.

"Timothy had come to my office today."

"Oh," she said. It was the least she expected. "But why to your office?"

"He said he wanted to visit our house but was a little hesitant because you might be hostile. He was all praise for our family and how he used to love visiting us, the dinners and the family gatherings. Most importantly, during our conversation, he said sincerely not once but twice - Natasha is a good girl, uncle, please take care of her."

"..."

"Having finished his masters, he had a lot to share about his one and a half years of life in Melbourne. He looked different and was not alone but with an Australian girl."

"Pa, shall we listen to the evening news?" she asked a little hesitantly when her father asked with a slight amusement, "Since when have you started listening to evening bulletin?" She just gave an awkward laugh.

"Always remember that your well being is the most precious, Natasha."

"But, why do you say that now, pa?"

"You must stay strong irrespective of any ups and downs. Timothy introduced that girl as his girlfriend, but only towards the end of the conversation. It was shocking to me." He looked at Natasha's face searchingly.

Before alighting near her workplace, Natasha said, "I knew all these months back. Don't worry pa; I will be quiet fine," as put her head on his shoulder and patted him.

Smiling she waved and walked away checking her mobile. She didn't turn to look at him gazing at her with awe.

She read the message that was from *Barbara: Extremely sorry Natasha. I tried very hard to convince Susan last night. She said that she does not believe in having any steady at all. Although she thinks you are a good person, she is not interested in you beyond just friendship and told me to tell you not to disturb her.*

With huge uncontrollable drops of tears, involuntarily stroking her head with her fingers, Natasha turned to look behind, but her father's car was not in sight, and darkness had swallowed the residues of the daylight entirely.

***

Acknowledgments

Sincere thanks to National Library Board of Singapore for having nurtured the voracious reader in me and especially to Bharathi Moorthiappan for the inspiration of the metaphor of Gandhi.

Thanks to the Chitran Raghunath, whose Art for the cover has added value to the book. I am honoured to have had Mrs. Lalitha Menon, retd. Professor and HOD from Calicut, Kerala, India as my first reader. Special thanks to her. Sincere thanks also to Angela Leong, Valerie Dümpelmann, Liu Fang, Sascha Ebeling, P.Muralidharan, and Sredhanea Ramakrishnan

Grateful to all those who continued with their encouragement in to help me retain my creative spirits in one way or the other - my three dear siblings, N.Srinivasan, N.Ramakrishnan and Usha, and my sisters-in-law Poornima and Subhashini, my friends Mitali Chakravarty, Madhumita, Nirmala, Usha Ramachandran, Radha Sriram, Aruna Srinivasan, Lakshmi Bala, Tulsi Gopal, Padma Aravind, and Revathy.